Even Batman Can't Hide from the Past...

MASK OF THE PHANTASM
BATMAN™
THE ANIMATED MOVIE

A Novelization by Andrew Helfer

Based on an original story by Alan Burnett

A BANTAM BOOK

New York · Toronto · London · Sydney · Auckland

RL 4, 008–012
BATMAN: MASK OF THE PHANTASM, THE ANIMATED MOVIE
A Skylark Book / January 1994

Skylark Books is a registered trademark of Bantam Books,
a division of Bantam Doubleday Dell Publishing Group, Inc.
Registered in U.S. Patent and Trademark Office and elsewhere.

Based on the original story by Alan Burnett

BATMAN and all related characters, slogans, and indicia are
trademarks of DC Comics.

Batman created by Bob Kane

ISBN: 0-553-48174-6

Published simultaneously in the United States and Canada. This
book is intended for sale only in the United States of America,
its territories and dependencies, the Republic of the
Philippines, and Canada.

Bantam Books are published by Bantam Books, a division of Bantam
Doubleday Dell Publishing Group, Inc. Its trademark, consisting of the words
"Bantam Books" and the portrayal of a rooster, is Registered in U.S. Patent
and Trademark Office and in other countries. Marca Registrada. Bantam
Books, 1540 Broadway, New York, New York 10036.

PRINTED IN THE UNITED STATES OF AMERICA

1   3   5   7   9   10   8   6   4   2

OPM

For The Other Robbin

CHAPTER 1

Chuckie Sol never smiled. Not even if he had a good reason. Chuckie had a reputation to maintain. If he smiled, his employees might think he was a nice guy. A regular joe. One of the boys. And that was the last thing Chuckie Sol wanted.

Chuckie Sol was a dangerous man. Every member of Gotham City's underworld knew it—and that was fine with Chuckie. Over the last decade, he'd made a fortune in crime. And as long as he managed to avoid getting caught, he was happy. But he never showed it. Because as long as Chuckie Sol never smiled, he would be feared.

Chuckie sat at the head of a long table in his penthouse office at the Shady Lady Casino, surrounded by four of his most trusted employees. Through the room-length window behind them, the Gotham City skyline glittered like a jewel in the night. But the men weren't there to take in the view. Instead, all eyes were focused on Chuckie as he placed a briefcase on the table and opened it.

The briefcase was filled with ten thousand one-hundred-dollar bills.

Angelo Dommer, Chuckie's number one man, lifted a single bill. He inspected it carefully, rubbing it between his fingers.

"Geez, Mr. Sol—I can't tell the difference."

"You'd need one of them neutron microscopes, Dommer," Chuckie said as he plucked the bill out of Dommer's hands and dropped it back into the brief-case. "It's identical down to Ben Franklin's stubble."

Chuckie shut the briefcase and eyed his four cronies. "I want it laundered through the casino at a half mil a week," he said through gritted teeth. "Three-quarter mil by March. Anybody got a problem with that?"

Chuckie's men knew better than to disagree with anything the boss demanded. In unison, they shook their heads. For them, trading counterfeit cash for the real thing was business as usual. They pushed their chairs back from the table, ready to head down to the casino to begin the job.

Just then a huge black form smashed through the window behind them. Shards of glass blew across the room as the men ducked out of the way. Then they turned to face whatever it was that had just crashed their private meeting.

Batman.

For a brief instant, nothing in Chuckie Sol's penthouse office moved. Chuckie and his men were awestruck. Batman stood before them, unmoving, his cape billowing in the breeze. Then Batman's eyes narrowed, his mouth tightened, his hands slowly balled into fists. In the silence of the penthouse, the tiny gestures screamed louder than words.

Max Doody was the first to try his luck. He leaped toward Batman, fists swinging. But Batman effortlessly ducked out of the way, countering Doody's feeble attack with a roundhouse punch that lifted Doody off his feet and slammed him back along the length of the table. Chuckie grabbed his briefcase and hugged it to his chest. He wanted to run, but his feet wouldn't cooperate.

As Chuckie stood frozen in fear, Dommer and a thug named Boris pulled their guns and began firing. An instant later, Batman tossed a Batarang that knocked the gun out of Boris's hand and then traveled on to crack Dommer on the head. Both thudded to the ground as Sammy Slick, Chuckie's top enforcer, appeared at the far end of the long table opposite Batman.

As Slick raised his gun, Batman ducked under the table. Adjusting his aim, Slick began firing his gun into the table. As the bullets rained down from above, Batman hefted the table up, smashing it into Slick's face. Now there was nothing between Batman and his goal: Chuckie Sol.

For a moment, their eyes locked. Chuckie still could not move—but his teeth chattered as Batman stepped forward. He was helpless. Then Chuckie saw Boris rise and begin to sneak up behind Batman. As Batman spun to face Boris, Chuckie's legs began to move. Somehow, the spell of fear had been broken. And Chuckie wasn't about to pass up an opportunity to escape. The last thing he heard before slamming the penthouse door behind him was Boris hitting the ground.

Chuckie raced down the stairs to the thirty-second floor. Here, a skybridge connected the Shady Lady Casino to a vast parking garage across the street. Chuckie bounded across the bridge and entered the dimly lit garage. The level was empty, except for Chuckie's car at the far end. If he could make it to the car, he'd be home free. Chuckie picked up the pace, running faster and faster toward the car—but stopped dead in his tracks when he noticed a cloud of smoke billowing up between him and his car. Then a figure appeared within the cloud.

The garage was poorly lit, and the figure was far away, so Chuckie couldn't be sure. But he *thought* it was Batman. As the figure came closer, it seemed to glide on the cloud that surrounded it. He didn't remember seeing any clouds tailing Batman up in his penthouse just before, but that didn't mean he didn't use them. Who knew what weird tricks the Bat had in that belt of his?

Chuckie wasn't taking any more chances. While the figure was still too far away to do anything about it, Chuckie pulled his gun, took careful aim, and fired. His first shot hit the figure dead-on. So did the second shot, and the third. But still it kept coming closer. Chuckie emptied all his bullets into the thing—and still it came. What was that guy made of?

Chuckie Sol didn't have to wait long to get his answer. A moment later he was face to face with the strange creature. And now Chuckie could see that it wasn't Batman.

He didn't think it was possible, but this black hooded figure, with a skull-like face, was more frightening than Batman ever was. Chuckie was terrified—and his fear grew when the creature spoke.

"Chuckie Sol," it said in a haunting whisper, "your angel of death awaits."

Chuckie stepped back as the ghoul moved forward. He wanted to shoot the thing but remembered his gun was empty. Instead, he swung at the figure with his gun. Chuckie's attacker lifted a ghostly arm, and Chuckie felt a flash of pain as the gun was torn out of his hand. Chuckie looked toward the gun on the ground—and saw that it had been sliced in half!

"Wh-who are you? Whaddaya want?" Chuckie stammered.

In response, the figure pointed its arm at Chuckie. There was a deadly steel blade attached to the end of the arm. "I am Phantasm," it said, "and I want *you,* Chuckie-boy."

As Phantasm raised the blade over Chuckie's head, Chuckie ran. In a moment, he was behind the wheel of his car. Out of breath and full of fear, he fumbled with the keys. Finally he managed to start the engine. And not a moment too soon: Phantasm was coming straight at him. But this time, Chuckie was prepared.

Chuckie snapped the headlights on and revved the car's engine. Then he slammed his foot on the gas. Tires screeched as the car took off—set on a collision course with Phantasm.

The car bore down on Phantasm, but just as it was about to hit the black-shrouded figure, Phantasm leaped up onto the hood of the car and plunged a razor-sharp, bladed hand through the windshield. Each swipe of the blade came closer to Chuckie's head. Chuckie dodged right, then left, but he knew he couldn't avoid the deadly blade much longer. He turned the steering wheel to the right and the car swerved, tumbling Phantasm to the ground.

Chuckie sighed in relief as he sped through the

garage. Through the rearview mirror he could see Phantasm on the ground, growing smaller as the car sped away.

Moments ago, all Chuckie Sol had wanted was to escape with his life. But now, seeing Phantasm lying there helplessly, Chuckie had another idea. *The creep just tried to kill me,* Chuckie thought, an evil sneer coming to his lips. *Well, now it's my turn.*

Again, Chuckie turned the steering wheel, U-turning the car so that it faced Phantasm. Then Chuckie hit the gas.

The car barreled down toward Phantasm, faster and faster. Chuckie's eyes glowed with anticipation. Before he even realized it, he began to smile. *Why not,* he thought. *No one's here. And besides,* Chuckie reasoned, *I deserve this.*

As the car came closer, Phantasm rose, but instead of moving out of the way, it just stood there. An unearthly mist once again gathered around the ghostly figure's feet. "This time I got you," Chuckie began, but he stopped as Phantasm's arms swept upward and the sinister being disappeared into the cloud of smoke.

Chuckie's car was moving too quickly to avoid the cloud. Instead, it passed through, and when the car emerged from the other side, it was filled with smoke. It was so dense Chuckie couldn't see an inch in front of his face. He coughed as he waved his arms around, desperately trying to peer through the windshield. Once he could, he realized that he had been tricked.

The narrow driving lane abruptly ended twenty feet in front of Chuckie's car. Beyond it was space—and across the space, Chuckie could see the windows of the Shady Lady Casino building on the other side of the street. Chuckie screamed in terror and slammed on the brakes.

His car smashed through the garage's short retaining wall, sailed through the air and crashed through one of the Shady Lady's windows on the other side of the street.

From the thirty-second floor skybridge, Batman watched as the wreckage of Chuckie's car settled in the Shady Lady's window. *Chuckie Sol has taken his last ride,* Batman thought. *But what could have made him try such a daredevil escape?*

As Batman turned to take a closer look at the garage, he could already hear people shouting from inside the casino. "Look!" one shouted. "It's him! It's Batman!" Batman had been spotted. It was only a matter of minutes before the police would arrive, so he had to move fast.

He stepped down to the level where Chuckie's car had blasted off. Pieces of glass were scattered on the floor. Batman picked up a shard and examined it. It was coated with a smoky, grimy residue. Thinking it might offer some clue, Batman placed the shard in his utility belt. Then he heard footsteps.

A strange, shadowy figure was standing near the garage stairway. The figure stood perfectly still for a second, then turned and disappeared into the stairwell. Batman followed, noticing a trail of smoke in the stairwell leading up to the roof. Batman raced up the stairs, taking them three at a time. But when he got to the roof, it was empty. Somehow, Batman knew he was going to take the blame for this affair.

CHAPTER 2

"I'm telling you, my friends," Councilman Arthur Reeves declared to the pack of television and newspaper reporters gathered at the steps of City Hall, "it's vigilantism at its deadliest! How many times are we going to let this happen? How many times are we going to let Batman cross the line?"

On the fringes of the crowd, Police Commissioner James Gordon stood next to his chief detective Harvey Bullock and listened until he could stand no more. "I'm sorry, Councilman," he interrupted as he stepped next to Reeves. "You can't blame Batman for what happened to Chuckie Sol."

Reeves looked outraged. "Why not?" he asked. "He was there. He was after him. He's a loose cannon, Commissioner! And it's not just my opinion. A lot of people think Batman's as unstable as the crooks he brings in!"

Arthur Reeves turned to face the cameras, raising a fist for effect as he posed a final question, not to Commissioner Gordon, but to the people of Gotham City. "What kind of city are we running when we depend on the support of a potential madman?"

Far away, in the suburbs of Gotham City, hundreds of feet below the vast estate known as Wayne Manor, one man had a response for Councilman Reeves.

"Such rot," Alfred Pennyworth declared as he switched off the Batcave's television. He turned toward the man working intently at the lab table on the other side of the huge cave. "Why, you're the very model of sanity." Bruce Wayne didn't answer. His mind was focused on his work. "Oh, by the way," Alfred added, "I've pressed your tights and put away your exploding gas balls."

Bruce Wayne smiled but didn't look up. "Thank you, Alfred," he said as his butler joined him at the lab table.

"Might one inquire what this is?" Alfred asked, pointing at the object in Bruce's hand.

"A piece of glass," Bruce said as he placed the shard into a specially designed microscope. "I found it at the scene of the accident." An enlarged image of the glass appeared on a computer screen nearby. As Bruce tapped on the computer's keyboard, the magnification increased until he could see the chemical makeup of the greasy substance covering the glass.

"Hmm . . ." Bruce mused. "There's a chemical residue baked onto it. Some kind of dense long-chain polymer . . ."

"Of course," Alfred agreed, humoring his boss as he headed toward the spiral staircase that led up into Wayne Manor. Bruce had scheduled a party for the following evening, and Alfred had to prepare for it. He had more important things to do than stare at "dense long-chain polymers."

The twin-engine plane swooped down through the skies over Gotham City. Inside, a woman spoke on a cellular phone as she absently thumbed through the latest issue of *Fortune,* the one with Bruce Wayne on the cover.

"It'll be good to see you again, Arthur," she said.

On the other end of the connection, Arthur Reeves preened before a small mirror. "You too," he answered. "And don't worry about a thing. We'll clear up those old family finances. Don't forget, you've got a big-time councilman on your side."

The woman in the plane stared at Bruce Wayne's

picture as she spoke. "I can't believe it's been ten years." She sighed.

"Thinking of looking up old friends?" Reeves asked suspiciously.

The woman shook her head as if coming out of a daydream. "Ancient history," she mused, dropping the magazine into her seat pocket.

"That's encouraging," Reeves said, relaxed and happy again. "Then I'll see you soon." Reeves hung up the phone, blew himself a kiss in the mirror, and went off to prepare for the woman's arrival.

Wayne Manor stood on the outskirts of Gotham City, a huge beacon in the dark, stormy night. Like moths drawn to a flame, dozens of cars drove up to the brightly lit mansion. Millionaire Bruce Wayne rarely threw parties, but when he did, all of Gotham's elite turned out.

In a corner of the mansion's huge main ballroom stood the party's host, surrounded by three beautiful society women. Despite their beauty, he looked totally bored.

"Oh, come on, Bruce," the first chirped. "All alone in this big mansion. Haven't you ever thought of marriage?"

"Never say the 'M' word around Bruce," the second giggled. "It makes him nervous."

"What about the 'I' word?" the third asked.

"The 'I' word?" Bruce wondered aloud.

"Ingagement," the third answered. The group laughed as another woman approached. She carried a drink in her hand and didn't look too happy to see Bruce surrounded by his female friends.

"I'd watch out for Brucie if I were you, girls," she began. "First he wines you and dines you. Makes you think you're the only woman he's ever been interested in. And just when you're wondering where to register the china, he forgets your phone number."

Bruce smiled weakly for a moment—and then the woman threw her drink in his face. "That's Bruce Wayne's style," she concluded angrily. Then she spun on her heel and walked away.

As the other three women looked in embarrassment at the dripping wet playboy, Bruce excused himself and headed toward his study. On the way he bumped into Councilman Reeves.

"A friend in need?" Reeves asked smugly, handing Bruce a handkerchief.

Bruce forced a smile as he wiped his face. "So, Councilman," he said, "how goes the Bat-bashing?"

"Better than your love life," Reeves replied. "Really, Bruce, it's almost as if you pick them because you know there's no chance for a serious relationship."

Bruce wanted to tell the pompous politician to mind his own business, but he kept silent as Reeves continued. "At least that one girl—what was her name?"

Reeves snapped his fingers, as if trying to recall. "Anne, Andi . . . Andrea. Yes. Andrea Beaumont."

Bruce winced at the sound of the name. He'd almost managed to forget Andrea Beaumont, but his memories of her were never too far from his mind. Thanks to Reeves, they were starting to flood back.

Sensing he'd touched a nerve, Reeves continued, "Now, there was a sweet number. How'd you let her get loose?"

In response, Bruce took Reeves's sopping wet handkerchief and stuffed it into Reeves's jacket pocket. Then he walked off, passing Alfred as he entered his study.

The room was dark, lit only by the occasional lightning that flashed through the study's huge windows. Bruce stood before the fireplace and stared at the portrait hanging over the mantelpiece. The painting was of Thomas and Martha Wayne, Bruce's parents. They had been murdered when Bruce was just a child, and their deaths had started him on a crusade that continued to this day. Whenever Bruce was troubled, he would stand before the portrait and seek his parents' guidance.

Now, as he looked up at the loving image of his parents, he recalled his first meeting with the woman whose memory so troubled him now. . . .

CHAPTER 3

Ten Years Ago.

In a strange way, Bruce Wayne found the cemetery comforting. After four years of constant study in college, he'd recently returned to Gotham City. Now he was faced with an endless stream of parties, dinners, and get-togethers that never allowed him a moment's peace.

Bruce Wayne knew what he wanted to do with the rest of his life. He just wasn't sure how he was going to do it. And with all the social engagements he'd been subjected to, he doubted he would ever have enough time to himself to figure it out. So he decided to come here whenever he could; to stand before the grave of his mother and father, pay his respects, and silently ask for their advice.

As he laid a pair of roses at the foot of the grave, he heard a woman's voice nearby.

"That's right," the woman said. "And if Daddy gets any more protective, I might as well join the Young Republicans."

Bruce turned to see a woman standing a short distance away. Her back was to Bruce, and since there was no one else there, Bruce could only conclude that the woman was talking to herself. Bruce stepped closer as she continued.

"It's times like this I wish you were around to—" She stopped suddenly and turned to face Bruce. "Yes?" she inquired.

"Excuse me," Bruce stammered. He was struck by her beauty. "I thought you were saying something. To me, I mean."

"No," the woman answered, then turned abruptly away.

"O-kay," Bruce said uncomfortably. He'd interrupted something and figured he'd better leave.

From the corner of her eye, the woman spotted Bruce walking off. A mischievous gleam appeared in her eye. She looked at the gravestone at her feet and smiled.

"You know who that was?" she asked, just loud enough for Bruce to hear. "Bruce Wayne. You know, Wayne Enterprises. I've seen him on campus. Very moody. Cute, though."

Bruce couldn't help himself. Again, he stopped to

listen. And again, when she turned to face him, she looked somewhat displeased. "Yes?" she said.

"I heard my name," Bruce stammered. "I thought—who are you talking to?"

The woman pointed to the gravestone. "My mother," she said.

"Oh," Bruce replied, embarrassed. "I didn't mean to—"

"That's okay," the woman said. "We're done. Mom doesn't have much to say today."

Bruce rolled his eyes. This was too much. The woman noticed the gesture and frowned. "Hey," she said, "I'm not the only one who talks to their loved ones, you know."

"I didn't say anything," Bruce said defensively. When she started walking toward the cemetery parking lot, Bruce trotted to keep up with her.

"It's just that when I talk to her out loud," the woman continued, "I can imagine how she'd reply. I can hear her as if she's right there."

Bruce understood, all too well. "I talked to my parents once," he said, growing solemn. "I made a vow. A secret vow."

Now it was the woman's chance to roll her eyes. "Oooh," she purred with a touch of sarcasm. "A man of mystery. So tell me," she said as she opened her car door, "have you kept your vow?"

Bruce rubbed his chin. "So far," he smiled, as the woman started the convertible's engine.

In response, the woman smiled and extended her hand. "Andrea Beaumont," she said.

"Bruce Wayne," he began—but Andrea pressed her foot to the gas and drove out of the cemetery, leaving Bruce alone. He smiled to himself at the thought of running into Andrea Beaumont again.

That night a full moon hung in the sky over Gotham City. Conditions were perfect for Bruce to begin a trial run for what he hoped would become a career in crime fighting. Dressed in black, he used a hook and rope to swing from skyscraper to skyscraper, patrolling the city, looking for trouble.

Soon he found it. Staring down onto a shipping dock from the ledge of a skyscraper, Bruce saw a group of men loading merchandise into the back of a large truck. He checked his watch: 3:00 A.M. It was too late at night—or too early in the morning—for normal deliveries. When he spotted a security guard tied up in a corner, Bruce knew it was time to go into action. He rolled his cap down over his face. It had two holes for his eyes and a third for his mouth. In the moonlight, he looked like a ninja warrior. As he prepared to descend from the rooftop, he hoped he would perform like one.

In the alley, the three burglars continued to load merchandise into the truck. Boxes brimmed out the back as one of them raised a walkie-talkie to his lips. "Okay, Skaz," he said. "We're done shopping."

At the mouth of the alley, the burglar named Skaz stood watch. "All clear here," he responded.

"Then let's blow this popstand!" the first burglar said as he joined his two partners at the back of the truck. They were just about to close the truck's rear doors when they heard a piercing cry from above. They looked up as a man dressed in black hurtled down toward them. He landed with a thud on top of the truck, then dived off the roof and somersaulted to the ground.

Bruce took a battle stance as he confronted the three burglars. "On your stomachs," he demanded. "Arms spread."

"Who is this clown?" one of the burglars asked. The first burglar pulled out a crowbar and slapped it menacingly against his open palm. "You heard Mr. Kung-fu, boys," he smirked.

"Yeah, I'm shaking," said the second burglar as he and the third raised their guns and began to circle around Bruce. In response, Bruce pulled a pair of ninja throwing stars out of his belt and tossed them at the two gun-toting burglars. The stars struck the burglars' hands, knocking their guns away.

"Get him!" The burglar with the crowbar screamed as he charged toward Bruce. As the crowbar swung past, Bruce ducked under the burglar and smashed him in the jaw, knocking him out cold.

But Bruce's job was far from over. The second burglar crept up behind Bruce and grabbed him in a bear hug, while the third punched Bruce hard in the stomach. Bruce's body went limp. The burglar holding him tried to lift Bruce so his partner could take another swing. But just as he'd succeeded in lifting Bruce to his feet, Bruce jerked his head back into the burglar's face. The burglar hit the ground with a thud.

Two down, one to go, Bruce thought as the final burglar charged toward him. Bruce could see the murderous rage in the thug's eyes and knew he could use that to his advantage. Rage made a man careless and cocky. Anger dulled his reaction time. Sure enough, the burglar rushed forward, swinging wildly, and Bruce had no trouble knocking him out.

Bruce took a deep breath as he looked over the unconscious men around him. He smiled broadly. He'd done it! He'd stopped three criminals—and it was a piece of cake!

Bruce turned toward the security guard, who lay tied up near the warehouse entrance. But as he began to loosen the gag covering the guard's mouth, Bruce noticed the panic in her eyes. The guard was looking over Bruce's shoulder.

Bruce turned as Skaz, the burglar who had been guarding the alley, sprayed machine-gun fire toward Bruce. Bruce rolled, pulling the guard out of the path of the bullets. Skaz turned and jumped into the truck's cab. His buddies might be down for the count, Skaz thought, but that wouldn't prevent him from making a bundle on this haul.

Skaz started the engine and pulled the truck out of the alley. He smiled to himself. Soon he'd be rich. It hadn't been such a bad night after all.

Skaz was so busy thinking about how he was going to spend his money he didn't realize the truck's back doors had been left ajar. As the truck picked up speed, boxes began tumbling out the back and crashing into the street. Skaz also didn't notice that someone was chasing the truck, ducking out of the path of the boxes as they fell.

Before the truck could escape him, Bruce leaped toward it, managing to grab on to one of the swinging doors. Each time the truck turned, more boxes spilled out, narrowly missing Bruce. Slowly, Bruce began pulling himself up—but before he could get inside, the truck passed a patrolling police car.

Skaz kept his cool; passing a police car was nothing for him to worry about. As far as he was concerned, he looked just like any other trucker with a late-night delivery to make. But Skaz didn't know about the man dangling from the back of the truck—which alerted the cops to the fact that something was very wrong.

When the police turned on the siren and took off after the truck, Skaz glanced at the rearview mirror nervously. *What could have tipped them off?* he wondered. When the truck's rear door swung into view and Skaz saw the man dangling from it, he was stunned. He thought he had got rid of that creep back at the warehouse!

The police car pulled up alongside the truck, and the cops inside motioned for Skaz to pull over. When Skaz refused, the police car pulled ahead, hoping to cut the truck off. As soon as it was in front of the truck, Skaz stepped on the gas.

WHAM! The police car shuddered as the truck rammed it from the rear. *WHAM!* The truck hit the police car again. The car swerved sideways, kicking up smoke as it tipped onto its side. The truck smashed into the underside of the police car, effortlessly brushing it out of its path, leaving the cops inside helpless.

Bruce watched the police car shrink in the distance. Now it was all up to him. But he'd lost the advantage of surprise: Skaz knew he was here.

As the truck hurtled along the highway, Bruce finally managed to climb to the roof and crawl across the length of it. Then he stepped down onto the top of the cab. As the truck entered the Gotham Tunnel, Bruce removed a small hammer from his belt and smashed it against the truck's windshield.

Thousands of weblike lines appeared across the glass as the windshield cracked. Skaz couldn't see a thing. The truck swerved back and forth, scraping against the sides of the tunnel. Bruce was buffeted about, but he held on, determined to see this chase to its conclusion.

Suddenly, Skaz jammed his foot down on the brake. The wheels locked, the truck skidded—and Bruce was thrown forward, past the windshield and over the hood of the truck.

Skaz saw the man dressed in black fly past the cracked windshield. *He's probably lying on the ground in front of me right now,* Skaz thought. He smiled as he jammed his foot on the gas. "That's the end of him," Skaz muttered as the truck rolled off.

But Skaz didn't know that at the last second Bruce had grabbed the truck's grille. Now, instead of hanging from the back of the truck, he was hanging onto its front!

As the wind blew fiercely at his back, Bruce came up with a plan. Carefully, he reached into his belt and removed a handful of spiked steel balls. Then he tossed them under the truck's wheels.

BWOOM! The front tire exploded! Out of control, the truck swerved and tipped onto its side. Skaz was instantly knocked out—but Bruce was still conscious and hanging onto the grille for his life. The truck skidded along the road for what seemed like forever. Finally it slowed to a halt.

Bruce breathed a sigh of relief as he let go of the grille. He tried to stand up, but something held him in place. He craned his neck around—and realized the truck had come to rest just inches away from the side of a building. If the truck had skidded just another foot, Bruce would have been crushed! Instead, as he heard the sound of sirens approaching, Bruce managed to squirm free. Before the police arrived, Bruce had climbed up the wall of a nearby building and run off. The way he had handled himself tonight, he wasn't ready to reveal himself to anyone.

"I read about your anonymous exploits this morning," Alfred said as he approached Bruce with the morning's paper, "and I must say—are you sure you won't reconsider rugby?"

On the lawn in front of Wayne Manor, Bruce Wayne punched and kicked at the air, replaying his moves of the night before. "Sorry, Alfred," he said, his bandaged face a mask of concentration, "but the plan is working. I had the edge. I could feel it." He stopped and gazed intently at his faithful butler. "There was only one thing wrong. They weren't afraid of me. I've got to strike fear in them from the start."

Alfred nodded. He understood and was about to say so when he noticed someone approaching. "Pardon, Master Bruce," he said, "but we may want to postpone the shoptalk as it were. I believe you have a visitor."

Bruce turned to see Andrea Beaumont. "Hey, what

happened to you?" she asked as she touched the nasty bruise on Bruce's forehead. "Trip over some loose cash?"

Bruce turned away. He couldn't tell her what had happened last night. She'd never understand. How could *anyone* understand why he did these things? Without even bothering to explain, Bruce continued practicing his fighting moves.

"What is that?" Andrea asked, stepping directly in front of Bruce.

"Jujitsu," Bruce answered, thrusting his hand into the air. "It takes years to master—"

Without warning, Andrea grabbed Bruce's hand and pulled it. Bruce flipped forward and crashed to the ground. Andrea smiled. "Got a few moves of my own," she said.

Bruce rubbed his head, smiling. "Where did you learn—?"

"Miss Hovey's self-defense class for girls," Andrea said. She towered over him triumphantly.

But not for long. Suddenly, Bruce swept his leg under Andrea's feet. Andrea fell to the ground. She was helpless. "Nice footwork," Andrea smiled. "Can you dance too?"

Bruce Wayne looked deep into Andrea Beaumont's eyes. She had all the right moves. And she had exactly the right attitude. Maybe she was the one. Maybe she could understand him.

Maybe . . .

CHAPTER 4

In the darkened study, Bruce looked at the portrait of his parents and thought about Andrea Beaumont. "Ten years ago . . ." he mused. "It seems like only yesterday."

Alfred knocked on the study door and entered, clearing his throat to get Bruce's attention. "Excuse me, sir," he said, "but Miss Bambi is dancing on the piano."

Bruce turned from the painting and sighed. *Time to play the millionaire playboy again,* he thought. He straightened his tie, pressed back his hair, and followed Alfred out of the study and back to the party in progress.

The Gotham City cemetery was about as far from Wayne Manor as you could get and still be inside the Gotham City limits. As lively as Wayne Manor was tonight, that was how dead this place was—at least, that was what Buzz Bronski thought as his limousine entered the cemetery grounds.

Bronski had come to the cemetery to pay his respects to an old friend and business associate. The friend had met a tragic end just a few days before at the hands of Batman.

Buzz felt guilty for missing his pal Chuckie Sol's funeral, but it was just too dangerous for him to be seen there. Who knew who might have been there to scope out underworld types like himself. The press. The cops. The Feds. Even the Bat. Better to visit poor old Chuckie one-on-one. Nobody snoops on you at two in the morning.

Still, just to be on the safe side, Buzz had brought a pair of bodyguards along for the ride. As he opened the car door, one of them handed Buzz a wreath and a flashlight.

"You guys wait here," Buzz said as he walked off. This would only take a minute.

Soon Buzz found the gravestone. He stared at it a moment, then looked at the wreath in his hand. "Chuckie, Chuckie," he sighed as he tossed the wreath at the stone. "You always were such a loser." Then he returned to the path that led back to his car.

He had only walked a few steps when he heard something. Not a voice, exactly, but a sound that seemed to drift in on the wind. He listened. It sounded like . . . his name!

Startled, Buzz spun around, shining his flashlight over the dozens of gravestones littering the field about him. No one there—just an old hoot owl staring at him through the darkness.

Buzz was relieved. The last thing he needed was to come face-to-face with Batman. He turned back onto the path—and was confronted by a roiling cloud of smoke. He stared at it, frozen with fear.

"Buzz Bronski," the voice repeated, as the cloud parted before him, "your angel of death awaits." A steel-tipped hand swiped through the remainder of the smoke, revealing the eerie figure of Phantasm. The ghostly being stepped toward Buzz Bronski.

"Get away from me, you freak!" Buzz shouted as he stepped back and turned to flee in terror. Deeper and deeper into the cemetery Buzz ran, tripping over gravestones and staggering through twisting mazes of gnarled tree branches. He had to put some distance between him and the cloud of smoke that followed him until he could think of some way to defend himself.

Soon he found it—or more precisely, he *tripped* over it. As he fled the skull-faced creature, Buzz crashed into a dirt-filled wheelbarrow. As he fell, his flashlight flew out of his hand. It hit the ground and shattered. Even though he knew it wouldn't do him any good, Buzz groped along the ground to retrieve it. Then, in the moonlight, he spotted a deadly looking pick axe. He grabbed it and kneeled behind the wheelbarrow, waiting for Phantasm to appear before him.

"Time to pay for your sins, Mr. Bronski," a voice suddenly spoke out. Buzz gulped. The voice was coming from *behind* him! Buzz stood perfectly still for a moment. Then, in one motion, he lifted the pick axe high over his head, spun around, and charged toward the sound of the voice.

Phantasm was ready for him. As the pick came sailing down, Phantasm swiped a hand blade through the air. It connected with the pick, slicing it in half. The metal end sailed through the air, leaving Bronski holding a harmless stump of wood.

Again, Phantasm started to float toward the helpless gangster. "You always were a loser, Mr. Bronski," Phantasm said as Bronski ran deeper into the cemetery. He had no pick axe, no flashlight, nothing to help him either defend himself or escape. He squinted in the moonlight. All around him were gravestones and statues. Or were they statues? Could one of them be Phantasm? Was he about to run smack into his attacker? Buzz Bronski wasn't sure of anything anymore. The only thing he was certain of was that he was standing on solid ground.

And then that gave way too.

Buzz Bronski fell a total of six feet. His soft face slapped against mud when he landed. He was frightened. He was dazed. He had absolutely no idea where he was. And then he looked up. He was inside an eight-foot-long rectangular hole. On the ground above one end an eight-foot-tall marble angel looked down on him. Buzz gasped in horror as he staggered back to the other end of the hole. He'd fallen into an empty grave!

He was about to reach up, to try to lift himself out, when a cloud of smoke began billowing across the ground above him. He held his breath as the image of Phantasm formed out of the smoke on the far side of the grave.

Phantasm looked down on Bronski but said nothing. There was no need. Bronski knew his goose was cooked. In desperation, he turned and ran the short distance to the end of the grave where the statue stood. He reached up to the edge of the grave and began clawing at the earth, trying to grab hold of anything that would help him get out. Clods of mud came loose from under the statue's base as Bronski tried to scramble up the wall. And still Phantasm did nothing. The ghostly creature just stood there, as though waiting for something to happen.

Bronski continued trying to paw his way out of the hole, but it was no use. All he'd succeeded in doing was digging away the dirt around the base of the statue. He looked back toward Phantasm at the opposite end of the grave—but Phantasm had disappeared yet again. This time, however, Phantasm quickly reappeared next to the statue. "Farewell, Mr. Bronski," Phantasm said before vanishing in a cloud of smoke.

Bronski scratched his head, confused. *That's it?* he wondered. *That ghoul's gonna leave me in a grave?* Bronski chuckled to himself. Maybe Phantasm planned to *starve* him to death!

Then Bronski noticed something strange. A finger-like stream of smoke was winding itself around the base of the stone angel. Slowly the statue began to tilt forward. Slowly it began to fall toward Bronski. Bronski screamed in terror as it tilted closer and closer toward him. There was nowhere to run. No place to hide. What could Buzz Bronski do?

Buzz Bronski kissed the angel.

A short time later, Bronski's two bodyguards came looking for their boss. After searching through the graveyard for an hour, they came upon a curious sight. A marble angel had fallen face first into an open grave. One of the bodyguards shined his flashlight into the hole—and that's when they noticed their boss.

"Oh, man," one said as they turned away in horror. As they walked back to the car, one man spotted a shadowy figure standing next to a gnarled tree in the moonlight. He cocked his gun and began firing at it.

The shadowy figure turned and fled, leaving the bodyguards to draw their own conclusions. "It's the Bat," one said. "It's the stinkin' Bat."

Thick iron bars covered every window of the nineteenth-century brownstone in Gotham City's fashionable Upper East Side, making it obvious that whoever owned the place wanted to keep any uninvited visitors out. A single light shined through the bars on the morning following Buzz Bronski's death.

Inside, a painfully thin old man sat in a big comfortable chair, stirring a spoon in his morning cup of tea. He reached for the morning paper as he brought the cup to his lips.

The headline made his blood run cold. SECOND GANGSTER SLAIN! it screamed.

The man's eyes widened with terror and recognition when he saw the photograph of Buzz Bronski. It couldn't be! His eyes darted over the page before focusing on the photo of Batman. Below the photo was the question "Has Batman Gone Bats?"

The cup of tea fell from the man's hand, shattering as it hit the ground. He began to wheeze and, rising from his chair, clutched his chest in pain. It was all too much. He couldn't breathe! Leaning against the chair for support, he reached for the tank of oxygen resting on the floor. Then, like a man dying of thirst, he pressed the mask against his nose and lips and took big greedy gulps of the life-giving oxygen.

Soon the tightness around his chest began to fade. Trembling, he sat back in his chair, exhausted from his ordeal, and stared at the newspaper lying on the floor. The picture of Batman seemed larger than life. It filled up his field of vision, sending chills down his spine. He kicked it aside and shook his head in despair.

Sal Valestra was a man with a problem.

CHAPTER 5

Councilman Arthur Reeves was angry. But his anger was kind of amusing, Commissioner Gordon thought as the councilman paraded back and forth in front of Gordon's desk at police headquarters.

"What do you mean you won't?" Reeves protested. "You have to go after him!"

Gordon shook his head. "He didn't do it." He rose from his desk and slid a pile of Batman-related newspaper clippings off the desktop. "It's garbage, Mr. Reeves," Gordon said as the clippings dropped into the wastepaper basket. "Batman does not kill—period."

On the ledge outside Gordon's office window,

Batman stood and listened. He smiled to himself. Besides Alfred, there was only one man in Gotham he could depend on. And right now, Jim Gordon was doing a pretty good job of defending him. Batman listened as Gordon continued.

"You get him," Gordon told Reeves as he pointed toward the door. "I'll have no part of it." Reeves sneered and marched out of Gordon's office.

Detective Harvey Bullock and two uniformed Gotham City policemen stood waiting in the reception area outside. Reeves smiled at them as he confidently squeezed a blast of breath spray into his mouth. "Well, gentlemen," he smiled, "any ideas?"

That night, the Bat-Signal appeared in the sky over Gotham. By now the sight of the signal had become familiar, both to the citizens of Gotham and to the man whose attention it was designed to attract. What was different from usual was the group of men who had lit the beacon and who were now standing atop police headquarters waiting for Batman to appear. Usually, Jim Gordon alone had the authority to flip the switch that turned on the Bat-Signal. But now Arthur Reeves and Harvey Bullock stood by the signal, waiting for something to happen.

Harvey Bullock glared at his watch. Ten minutes, and still no sign of the Bat. Reeves smiled. *He'll*

come, he thought to himself. *Sooner or later, he'll come. . . .*

On the outskirts of Gotham City, Batman saw the signal. But he knew who had lit it and wasn't interested in stepping into their ambush. If they wanted to catch him, fine. But they were going to have to think up something better than this. Besides, he reasoned, as the Batmobile roared away from the city toward the Gotham City cemetery, he had more important things to do.

Soon Batman stood over the grave of Chuckie Sol. He knelt down to feel the ground around the headstone. "There appears to be some chemical residue on the lawn," he mused as he ran his fingers over the grass. "It could match the traces I found on the glass."

While searching around the graveyard for other clues, Batman suddenly realized he had wandered into a familiar section of the cemetery. He walked up a short hill, his pace quickening as he realized his destination.

Batman stood before the grave of his parents, his head bowed respectfully. *Funny,* he thought, *how I always seem to come back here.* He'd visited hundreds of times before, but never wearing the costume he'd designed to wage the war on crime that he fought in his parents' name. He hoped that somehow they could see him standing here and prayed they would be proud of him. He prayed for something else too— and an instant later, his prayers were answered.

"You'd think they could afford a weed eater," the woman's voice said. "Sorry, Mom, but the whole world's going to seed."

Batman turned. Could it be?

It was! Andrea Beaumont! He began to step forward—but then he caught himself. *I'm not Bruce Wayne now,* he thought. *I'm* BATMAN! If Andrea saw him like this . . .

He stepped back, and as he did, his foot crunched a small branch on the ground.

Startled, Andrea turned and came face-to-face with Batman. She raised a hand to her lips and opened her mouth to scream. *She's afraid of me,* Bruce realized. *And why shouldn't she be?*

This wasn't the way he wanted it to happen. He'd dreamed of seeing her again, yearned to hold her. But as Bruce Wayne, not Batman. As Andrea watched in stunned silence, Batman turned and fled.

Andrea ran after him but stopped dead in her tracks when she passed a familiar gravestone. The sight of the stone was even more jarring than the sight of Batman. She looked at the name chiseled upon the face: WAYNE.

"No. It can't be . . ." she murmured, and looked

up at Batman as he disappeared over the top of the hill. "Bruce . . ."

Andrea Beaumont seemed distracted as she sat down to dinner that night with Councilman Arthur Reeves at the exclusive Windows Over Gotham restaurant. The things she'd seen—and worse, the things she suspected—made her head spin. She was so lost in thought she hardly heard Reeves speak.

" . . . so I'm having the banker cut through some

red tape. He says you can roll your money into a higher-yield account."

Andrea blinked and shook her head dreamily. "Amount?" she wondered. "What amount?"

"I said *account*."

Andrea smiled sheepishly. "I'm sorry. I was just reminiscing."

Reeves smiled. He understood completely, or at least, he thought he did. "Hey," he said, "that's okay. You must have a lot on your mind." He turned to scan the elegant restaurant. "Remember this place?" A twinkle of nostalgia brightened his eye.

"Sure. You, me, and daddy used to come here all the time."

"How is the old guy?" Reeves asked. "You're still close, aren't you?"

Andrea smiled warmly. "Closer than ever."

"I'm sorry he couldn't make it into town this time," Reeves said with a smile that made it clear he wasn't sorry at all. Then he reached across the table and took Andrea's hand. "But then, I've always wished I could have some time alone with you."

Andrea glanced down at Reeves's hand, then looked at him and grinned. "Well," she said, "who knows what the future might bring?"

Across the street, from atop Gotham Cathedral's highest spire, Batman watched Councilman Reeves take Andrea Beaumont's hand. He sighed. *Was it so long ago?* he wondered. Memories flooded back, as hard and cruel as the rain that fell from the Gotham City skies. . . .

CHAPTER 6

Ten Years Ago.

This was it. The day Bruce and Andrea had been waiting for: opening day of the Gotham City World's Fair. The newspapers proclaimed that the fair would offer a glimpse into Gotham's future—and since Bruce and Andrea were planning to share a future with each other, they decided to preview it together.

Who would have thought the future would be so much fun! The fair was as much a playground as anything else. Bruce and Andrea entered through the main gates and headed toward the central plaza. The fair's centerpiece, a sculpture of a futuristic-looking rocket ship propped up against a huge ringed planet, stood in the middle of the plaza. Bruce and Andrea stared at the structure in awe until a voice boomed over the public address system:

"Welcome to a dream of the future, a bright tomorrow filled with hope and promise for all mankind. This is a vision of the shimmering utopia where we shall all spend the rest of our lives . . ."

Andrea and Bruce smiled at each other as they headed toward the fair's first attraction: the World of the Future ride. They scrambled aboard one of a train of futuristic cars designed to take them on their tour.

Robotic actors sang a cheerful song as the car drove through a miniature model city of the future. Tiny autogyros flew through the air, buzzing over their heads, until they reached the next part of the exhibit: the House of the Future.

The futuristic home was complete down to the last detail. Time-saving appliances, space-age furniture— it even had a robot family! A male robot watched a television that floated in midair as he waved at the visitors, a female robot stood behind a kitchen table, endlessly chopping vegetables, and a robotic dog yapped happily, running alongside Bruce and Andrea's car as it exited the House of the Future exhibit.

Next, the car took them to the Hall of Transportation. Andrea looked around in awe at the futuristic planes hovering in the air around them. "Do you think we'll really see any of this in our lifetime?" she asked Bruce.

But Bruce wasn't paying attention. Something had caught his eye, and as if in a daze, he jumped off the train and approached it to get a closer look. Curious, Andrea followed.

A bullet-shaped, jet-powered car with a dramatic fin protruding from the tail rested on a rotating platform in front of them. A sign above it read: THE CAR OF THE FUTURE. *Amazing,* Bruce thought. *This is the one.*

"Bruce?" Andrea interrupted. "Bruce, I'm talking to you."

Bruce tore his eyes away from the magnificent vehicle to face Andrea. "Oh," he stammered. "I'm sorry, Andi. My mind was on . . . something else . . ."

"Like what?" Andrea asked, taking Bruce's arm and leading him away from the amazing automobile.

"Oh, just . . . you know," Bruce answered, waving his hand at his surroundings. "The future."

Andrea raised an eyebrow. "Anyone's in particular? Or just the generic brand?"

Bruce smiled nervously as he and Andrea walked through the parking lot toward the limousine waiting to take them home. "You know . . ." Bruce muttered.

Andrea stopped in front of the car. "No, I don't. When was the last time you talked to *me* about your plans?"

Alfred appeared and opened the car door. Andrea turned to Bruce. "You know," she said, "Dad's been wanting to meet you."

Bruce gulped. "Oh, yeah?"

"But I told him you're not up to it yet."

Bruce gritted his teeth, but the words came out anyway. "I can meet him."

Andrea's arms flew around Bruce's neck. She pulled him close and kissed him. "Great!" she said. Then she hopped into the car. "I'll call him right now!"

While Andrea dialed her father on the car phone, Bruce cast an anxious glance at his butler. "What the heck am I doing, Alfred?" he whispered. "This isn't part of the plan! I must be going nuts!"

Alfred shook his head to correct his employer. "If I may be so bold, Master Bruce—I'd say quite the opposite."

Later that afternoon, Carl Beaumont sat in his office discussing business with Arthur Reeves, his young assistant. *Reeves was a smart young man,* Beaumont thought, *full of drive and ambition.* He would go far within Beaumont's organization. Beaumont suspected that one day Arthur Reeves would be a very wealthy man. But deep down, Carl Beaumont wondered if money was what Arthur Reeves was really after.

"Knock, knock."

Beaumont looked up as his daughter Andrea

entered his office with a handsome, dark-haired young man. Bruce seemed nervous as he shyly followed Andrea in.

"Well." Beaumont smiled. "This is a most pleasant interruption." He stood to shake Bruce's hand. "At last I meet the elusive Bruce Wayne."

"Nice to meet you, sir," Bruce said meekly.

"Sir?" Beaumont repeated, taken aback. "Don't be so formal, Bruce. Andrea's told me so much about you—I feel like we're practically family."

Andrea blushed. "Daddy . . ." she groaned uncomfortably.

From the corner of the office, Arthur Reeves conspicuously cleared his throat. "Don't mind me, sir," he said, stepping toward the door. "I was just leaving."

"Oh, I'm sorry," Beaumont said. In the excitement of seeing his daughter, he'd completely forgotten his assistant. "This is Arthur Reeves, one of the hot young turks from my legal department."

Reeves and Bruce shook hands. "Arthur is someone you should get to know," Beaumont added.

A long, dark limousine pulled up to the curb in front of Carl Beaumont's office building. A tall, sharp-featured driver emerged and walked around the front of the car to open the door for his boss.

Clouds of cigar smoke wafted into the open air as

the passenger emerged. He dropped his cigar to the ground and crushed it with his foot, then headed for the entrance.

Back in Beaumont's office, Bruce and Carl Beaumont were getting to know each other.

"I hope we're not interrupting anything," Bruce said.

"Not at all," Beaumont replied with a dismissive wave of his hand. "I'm never too busy for my Andi and her friends. I tell you Bruce, I do a lot of financial planning. When it comes to money, you can't take the future for granted. But all the money in the world means little if you don't have loved ones to share it with. Nothing's more important than family."

Bruce smiled broadly. He couldn't agree more. He was about to say as much when Beaumont's secretary appeared at the door.

"Excuse me, sir," she said nervously, "but there's a Mr. Valestra here to see you. He says he has an appointment."

Bruce watched carefully as Andrea's father seemed to shrink before his very eyes. Somehow, at the mention of the name Valestra, Carl Beaumont had lost the inner strength Bruce immediately sensed in the man.

Beaumont cleared his throat. "If Mr. Valestra says

he has an appointment, Virginia, then Mr. Valestra has an appointment."

An instant later, a tall, powerful-looking man swaggered into Carl Beaumont's office. He stepped behind Beaumont's desk and plopped down into the chair as if he owned the place.

"That's what I like about your pops, kiddo," Valestra sneered. "He knows his priorities."

Valestra flipped open a box on Beaumont's desk, removed a cigar, and lit it. *Who is this guy?* Bruce wondered as Valestra confidently blew smoke rings in the air. Hurriedly, Beaumont ushered Bruce and Andrea out of his office.

Moments later, the two were back on the street. Bruce shoved his hands deep in his pockets and shivered. "Is my shirt too big," he asked Andrea, "or is that my flesh crawling?"

"Valestra has that effect on people sometimes," Andrea agreed, as she and Bruce walked away from the building.

From the sideview mirror of Sal Valestra's limousine, the tall, sharp-featured driver watched as Andrea and Bruce walked away.

"Dad just counts their money," Andrea added in her father's defense. "They don't tell him where it comes from."

"It's not your father, Andi," Bruce tried to explain as the two wandered toward downtown Gotham. "It's—it's everything—I—"

Bruce stopped as he heard the sound of revving motorcycles.

"I said, hand over the cash box, man!" a voice suddenly shouted. Bruce turned.

A short distance away, under the Gotham Subway elevated train trestles, three motorcycle thugs were threatening a street vendor. The vendor fearfully hugged his cash box to his chest as he backed away from the trio.

One of the thugs got off his motorcycle and grabbed the old man by his collar, trying to shake the box loose. "Gimme," he hissed, "or so help me I'll mess up your face so bad you'll be breathin' outta the part in your hair!"

Seeing this wasn't going to be as easy as it first looked, the second biker approached. He removed a blackjack from his jacket as he walked over to assist his partner.

Bruce Wayne watched all this until he could watch no more. He motioned to Andrea. "Stay put," he said. "This could get serious."

Andrea tugged at his arm. "Bruce, no!" she cried desperately. "Don't!"

Bruce's temper flared as he turned to face her. "What do you expect me to do?" he shouted angrily. "Just stand here?!"

Andrea's eyes glistened tearfully as she touched Bruce's cheek. "Just come back to me in one piece," she sniffed. "Please." Bruce looked deep into her eyes a moment, then turned and ran.

As Bruce raced toward the thugs, the second biker slapped his blackjack across the helpless vendor's head. The old man crumpled, dropping his cash box, which slid across the pavement. As the first biker thug kneeled to retrieve it, Bruce dived toward him and knocked him to the ground.

Enraged, the second biker charged at Bruce with his blackjack swinging. Bruce bobbed and weaved between the biker's flailing arms, looking for the right moment to make his move. As the biker's hand swept wide over Bruce's head, Bruce reached toward his chest and grabbed a handful of the biker's jacket. Then he heaved the biker into the air, flipping him across the street.

Now Bruce turned his attention to the first biker, who had risen to his feet.

For a moment, Bruce and the biker simply stared at each other. Then, instead of resuming the fight, the biker turned and staggered back toward his motorcycle. There, a third motorcycle thug sat on a bike, watching. *They're nothing but cowards,* Bruce thought as the two bikers kick-started their engines and began driving off.

Bruce watched as the bikers sped into the distance. But as he retrieved the vendor's cash box he heard the sound of motorcycle engines approaching. Bruce looked up. The bikers were returning—and this time, they had weapons. The first biker swung a chain over his head as he approached. The other biker had produced a baseball bat. "Better have your insurance paid up," the biker shouted at Bruce as he drove toward him.

On the sidewalk, Andrea watched in horror as the biker with the chain revved his engine and drove toward Bruce. *What was Bruce doing?* she wondered. He was just standing there. Waiting. Not moving a muscle. Like a frightened deer caught in the headlights! He had to get out of the way! He had to run— before it was too late!

An instant later, Bruce *did* start to run. But much to Andrea's dismay, he began running *toward* the motorcycle. Andrea raised her hand to her mouth in fear—but just as Bruce was about to crash head-on into the motorcycle, he jumped onto the bike's front fender. The motorcycle thug barely had time to understand what was happening as Bruce landed a solid punch on his nose.

Out of control, the motorcycle skidded out from under Bruce and the biker, sending them both flying through the air. The biker crashed to the ground in a heap—but Bruce had practiced moves like this hundreds of times before. He somersaulted through the air before gracefully landing on his feet right in front of the biker wielding the baseball bat!

As she watched, Andrea cried out. Bruce tried to ignore her, tried to focus on the immediate threat, but Andrea's last words to him filled his head:

"Just come back to me in one piece . . ."

His concentration broken, Bruce turned to glance back at Andrea just as the biker barreled in. His baseball bat splintered as it slammed into Bruce's stomach and knocked him to the ground.

In horror, Andrea rushed toward Bruce, who could hardly move. His chest felt as if it were on fire. His ribs were badly bruised . . . maybe broken. He was in no condition even to attempt to prevent the two bikers from grabbing the vendor's cash box and driving off. He'd tried to do good. He'd tried to set right the wrongs of criminals. He'd tried to keep the vow he'd made to his parents long ago. He'd tried . . . and failed.

As the bikers rode off, Bruce shakily rose to his feet. Andrea was by his side. "Thank God you're all right," she whimpered as she buried her head in his shoulder. "I was so frightened." She tenderly touched his bruised cheek. "Come on. Let me have a look at you—"

Irritated, Bruce brushed her hand away. "Andrea— please—" he began, but he quickly realized that she couldn't understand—that she'd *never* understand.

And so, Bruce Wayne simply walked away.

That night, Bruce sat in his study, a pencil and sketch pad in his hand. For the past few hours he'd been drawing designs for costumes. Something for him to wear when he went to do battle with Gotham's underworld. It had to be something frightening— something that would spook the criminal element right away, that would make them feel they weren't dealing with something entirely human. He needed to have an edge over the criminals he'd be fighting— and a good costume would give him one instantly.

Still, this drawing wasn't what he was looking for. He tore it off the pad, crumpled it into a ball, and tossed it into the fireplace.

Bruce watched as the ball burst into flames. Although his mind was on his mission, his heart was somewhere else. "What am I still doing this for?" he wondered aloud. He turned from the fireplace and gazed out the window into the stormy night. "It's gotta be one or the other. I can't have it both ways. I can't put myself on the line as long as there's someone waiting for me to come home."

"Miss Beaumont would be glad to know you feel that way, Master Bruce," Alfred suddenly said. Bruce turned toward his butler. "She's holding on line one."

Bruce stared with dread at the telephone on his desk. Alfred lifted the receiver off the hook and extended it toward him. Bruce reached out to take it—but then dropped his hand and sadly shook his head. "Alfred . . . I can't . . . not now."

Alfred looked at Bruce uncomfortably. "But what shall I say?"

"I don't know," Bruce replied, his face filled with frustration. "I just don't *know*!" Angrily, he slammed his fist against the wall and stormed out of Wayne Manor into the rain.

Bruce Wayne knew there was only one place for him to go now. Since he'd met Andrea, everything was different. Long ago, he'd vowed on his parents' grave never to stop fighting crime. But back then, he was filled with rage. When his parents had been killed, he'd found himself suddenly alone in the world. Without them, life had no meaning. And as he stood in the driving rain before their grave, Bruce realized that it was the pledge itself that had filled up that part of his life left empty by the loss of his parents.

But now, something new had come into his life, pushing out his single-minded devotion to fighting crime. There was no other word for it: love.

Bruce knelt before his parents' grave. "It doesn't mean I don't care anymore," he whispered. "I don't want to let you down, honest, but it just doesn't hurt so bad anymore."

The rain splashed down on the gravestone, leaving trails like tears along it. "I know I made a promise," Bruce implored, "but I didn't see this coming. I didn't count on being happy. Please tell me it's okay."

As if in answer, lightning flashed above the tombstone, lighting up the whole graveyard. In the brief, brilliant light, Bruce noticed a shadow falling across the gravestone. "Maybe they already have," a familiar voice said. Bruce turned to see Andrea.

"Maybe they *sent* me." For a moment, Bruce and Andrea faced each other in the pouring rain. Then Bruce rushed forward to embrace the woman he loved.

CHAPTER 7

Atop Gotham Cathedral, Batman shook his head to clear away the painful memories. His time with Andrea Beaumont had come and gone; the way she looked at Arthur Reeves while the councilman held her hand proved that. Ten years later, he was alone once again—and destined to be alone for as long as he lived. He bowed his head sadly just as the sound of a Police Patrol blimp filled the air. He watched it move across the sky and saw its searchlight approaching.

It was time for him to leave.

Arthur Reeves walked briskly down the street. The world was his. The press and half the police force were already in his pocket, and if he had his way, Andrea Beaumont would soon be joining them there.

Suddenly a long black limousine screeched to the curb alongside Reeves. The rear window rolled down to reveal the ancient, sickly face of Sal Valestra. Valestra looked up suspiciously at Reeves. "Get in," he croaked.

Reeves had no choice but to oblige. After all, Valestra was the boss. Reeves got in and sat down next to Valestra. He winced. Reeves was always uncomfortable around sick people, and Sal Valestra was one of the sickest men he'd seen. Ten years ago, Sal Valestra had been the strongest, most robust gangster Reeves knew. Now, thin, pale, and hunched over a portable oxygen tank, Valestra looked as if he might kick the bucket any second. And Reeves was looking forward to that moment.

"All I want to know," Valestra asked, "is if it's true. Is the Batman really hitting our people?"

Reeves nodded. "We have eyewitnesses."

Valestra looked visibly shaken. "Beautiful," he croaked. "That's just beautiful. Why? He never leaned on us before." Valestra put his head in his hands. "I'm too old for this," he grumbled.

"I suppose you could demand police protection," Reeves offered.

Valestra turned toward Reeves angrily. "What are you, a comedian?" he shouted. "This is the Batman we're talking about! A freak job!", Valestra wheezed. "He'll kill me!!" He began coughing now, a rasping, painful cough. Desperate and frightened, he fumbled for his oxygen tank and lifted the mask to his face, trying to catch his breath.

Reeves observed this with disgust. "Pull over," he told the driver. As the car came to a stop, Reeves got out. He looked back over his shoulder at Valestra. "It's not very healthy in here," he remarked and slammed the door behind him. *Valestra might be the boss,* Reeves thought as he walked down the street, *but in his condition, it wouldn't be for long.* It couldn't hurt to be a little rude . . . to a dead man.

Batman sat in front of the Batcave's huge super-computer, typing away at the keyboard. A few more entries and he'd have his answer. A moment passed, and a list of company names appeared on the monitor before him.

"O'Neil Funding Corp., Adams Tool & Die . . ." Batman smiled. "Ah . . . I should have known."

Alfred stood nearby, polishing the fencing swords in Batman's weapons collection. "Sir?" he inquired.

"Chuckie Sol and Buzz Bronski," Batman replied. "They have some history together. They were part-ners—in dummy corporations set up over ten years ago." Batman tapped a few more keys, and the list of companies was replaced by a shorter list of names. "The third director was one Salvatore Valestra."

Batman flipped the computer off and stood. "Sal's having company tonight," he said as he moved toward the Batmobile. "Don't wait up."

Alfred smiled. "Meaning, I trust," he said hopefully, "that once you're done with him, you'll be seeing her?"

Batman turned. "You think you know everything about me, don't you?"

Alfred crossed his arms on his chest. "I diapered your bottom," he grumbled. "I bloody well ought to. Sir."

Batman jumped into the Batmobile and revved the engine. "Well, you're wrong." He frowned. The Batmobile's engine roared as he drove off.

Batman had no problem breaking into Sal Valestra's brownstone. For all the thick iron bars framing each and every window, the lock on the front door was cheap and easy to pick. Batman simply walked up the stairs and into Valestra's study.

Valestra's desk was covered with business papers. Batman searched through them but found nothing suspicious. This didn't surprise him. He knew that criminal types like Valestra didn't survive long if they left incriminating papers lying about. But Batman also knew that even the cleverest criminals made mistakes.

With this in mind, Batman scanned the room. A series of photographs lined one wall. Batman examined each one carefully. Sometimes you can learn a lot about a man by the company he keeps. There was an image of a young Valestra with a beautiful woman. Another showed Valestra smiling alongside Gotham City Mayor Hill. It was the last photograph, however, that made Batman pause.

The black and white photograph must have been taken a decade earlier. It showed four men seated around a restaurant table. Each man smiled broadly. Despite the fact that they looked much younger, Batman recognized them all. First there was Valestra—with his tall, sharp-featured bodyguard in the background. Then there was Buzz Bronski. And Chuckie Sol.

And in the middle of the group of gangsters, a glass of champagne in his hand, was Carl Beaumont.

Batman's eyes narrowed. Ten years had passed since he'd seen Carl Beaumont's face—and he'd almost forgotten what had happened that last time. Now the memories rushed back . . .

CHAPTER 8

Ten Years Ago.

Bruce and Andrea strolled along the rocky path that wound down the hillside behind Wayne Manor. Andrea absently kicked at the pebbles as she walked, her head lowered sadly.

"My father's taking me away. It's some sort of hush-hush deal. He won't tell me a thing," she said, her voice cracking with emotion. "He won't even say when we'd be coming back."

Bruce put a hand on Andrea's shoulder, then held her close to him. "Will you at least let me *try* to talk you out of it?" he begged.

Andrea loosened herself from his grip and sat on a nearby rock. "Bruce . . ." she sniffed.

Bruce raised a hand to silence her. "Wait. Please,"

he began. Then he stopped. He started to speak again—then stopped. He opened his mouth—then closed it. *What was he trying to say?* Andrea wondered.

Then Bruce shoved his hands into his pockets. "Oh, never mind," he said, frustrated. "I'm no good at this." He removed a small, velvet-covered box from his pocket and handed it to Andrea. "Here, you'll get the idea." Then he got down on his knee and waited for Andrea to open the box.

Andrea looked at the diamond ring inside. Then, with tears of happiness brimming in her eyes, she threw her arms around Bruce's neck. "Of course I will," she sobbed. "I never thought this would happen."

Bruce took the box from her, removed the ring, and placed it on her finger. "I always felt like I'd thrown you a curve ball," she said. "Like you never knew what to do with me . . . 'cause I wasn't in the plan."

Bruce smiled. "You are now," he said gently. "I'm changing the plan."

He leaned over to kiss her but as their lips met, Bruce heard a strange chirping sound. He cocked his head to the side. The sound was getting louder. It wasn't a chirping any longer—now it sounded like a *screech. No*, Bruce thought as he listened, *make that* thousands *of screeches. But what could be making that kind of noise?* Bruce wondered.

Without warning, the crevice next to the rock Andrea had been sitting on erupted with an explosion of bats! Thousands of the black furry creatures poured out of the hole, blackening the sky and forcing Andrea and Bruce to stagger back.

Bruce raised a protective arm over Andrea and watched in awe as the swirling mass of bats rose up into the sky. *Is this a sign*? he wondered. *A sign of bad things to come*? He hugged Andrea close and shut his eyes tightly. He prayed it was not.

Hours later, Alfred drove Bruce's limousine up the narrow driveway that lead to Carl Beaumont's home. In the backseat, Bruce and Andrea were nervous. They were about to tell Carl Beaumont they were getting married. Neither Andrea nor Bruce were certain how he would react to the news.

As the limo passed Beaumont's study window, Andrea glanced inside. "Uh-oh," she said. "Looks like he's got company—business-type company."

Bruce looked toward the study window. Through the open blinds he could see the outlines of three men standing opposite Beaumont, who stood behind his desk. He glanced at Andrea and noticed her nervousness. "He doesn't usually have clients here," she said. "At least," she added as the limo pulled up to the front of the house, "not at this hour."

Bruce stepped out of the car and opened the door for Andrea. "Maybe we should wait until tomorrow before we give him the good news," she said uncertainly.

"Maybe," Bruce echoed.

Andrea guessed that meant Bruce agreed. "Good night, Bruce," she said, smiling. Then she walked up the stairs to the front door.

It wasn't until Bruce was back inside the car that he noticed the tall, sharp-featured man standing off to the side of the front door. Bruce watched as Andrea walked past without so much as a glance in the man's direction. He noticed the tall man wink at Andrea and smile slyly. But Andrea paid no attention to him. And as she slammed the front door shut, the man turned toward Bruce and sneered.

What a creep, Bruce thought as the limo pulled away.

The next morning, Bruce dropped a rope ladder down into the crack in the ground where the bats had emerged. With only a flashlight to guide him, he investigated for over an hour. When he climbed out of the crevice, Alfred was waiting for him. The butler looked troubled, but Bruce was too excited by his discoveries to notice.

"It's another cave, all right," Bruce exclaimed.

"Could be as big as the house, judging from the number of bats that came out of it!"

Alfred just shook his head as he handed Bruce a small box wrapped in paper. "This just arrived, sir," he said.

Bruce snatched the box from Alfred's hand and stared at it. He knew what it was. But what did it mean? Panicking, he tore off the paper wrapping. A small note was taped to the black velvet box.

Bruce couldn't believe what he was reading. "Left with Dad . . ." he mumbled. " . . . too young . . . need time . . . forget about me." It was over. She'd left him. There was nothing else for Bruce Wayne to do now— but what he had long ago vowed to do.

A few days later, the Gotham City Police started getting a series of strange confessions from criminals who had been attacked and beaten either during or shortly after committing crimes. Without exception, the criminals explained that they had been attacked by a horrifying batlike creature.

At first the police laughed these reports off. They were a bunch of fairy tales, created by criminals so they could cop insanity pleas. But as the number of reports doubled, then tripled, the police realized they had something very real on their hands.

For Bruce Wayne, the war had begun.

CHAPTER 9

Batman continued to stare at the photograph of Carl Beaumont and his underworld partners that hung on Sal Valestra's study wall. The ten-year-old memories it brought back made it almost painful to look at. But Batman had to look. This was what he had come here for. It was a clue. And no matter how unpleasant, it was his job.

He lifted the photo off the wall, tucked it under his cape, and left.

The Gotham World's Fairgrounds were in a state of disrepair. The fair had ended a decade ago, but instead of demolishing the dozens of rides and attractions, the city had decided to simply leave the exhibits in place. Then, when the future that the fair had predicted finally arrived, people could return to the site and see how close the fair had come to reality.

It was kind of sad, Sal Valestra thought as his car drove through the abandoned park. His own future, like the future imagined by the fair, had seemed so bright and hopeful ten years earlier. Now, as he rode past the Science Land and Technology of the Future exhibits, he realized that both he and Gotham City had fallen far short of their dreams.

But Sal hadn't come here to relive the past. He was here to meet someone. When the car came to a stop in the center of the main plaza, Sal got out and took a deep breath from his portable oxygen tank. *If there was just some other way,* he thought as his eyes nervously scanned the plaza. He shook his head sadly. *This was it,* he thought. *No other way.* He reached into the car and removed a small suitcase. Then he headed toward the World of the Future exhibit.

The huge robotic puppets dangling over the entrance to the World of the Future exhibit hadn't moved in over a decade. Once a shiny blue metal, they were now covered with ten years' worth of Gotham City grime and soot. Sal looked at them sadly—and they suddenly started to move! And sing! And then—*explode!*

Sal dropped to the ground when he heard machine-gun fire. Bullets were flying over his head and into

71

the singing robots, blowing them to pieces. When the shooting stopped, Sal wheezed in fear as he stared into the exhibit's darkened entrance.

The Joker stepped out of the shadows, a smoking machine gun in his hand. "I hate that song," he cackled. When he saw Sal lying on the ground he slapped his palms against his head. "Gasp! Can it be? Old Sallie 'The Wheezer' Valestra!"

Slowly, Sal stood, picking up the suitcase and oxygen tank he'd dropped when the shooting started. "Welcome, *paesan*'!" The Joker said, clapping Sal on the shoulders. "It's been a dog's age!"

Sal smiled nervously. "Hello, Joker," he said. "Didn't mean to drop by unannounced."

"Oh, Salvatore," The Joker leered, "why so formal? My house is your house!" Sal nodded his appreciation as The Joker continued. "So, what's an old-timer like you want with a two-timer like me?"

"Business," Sal replied as he stepped back toward one of the little cars that once conveyed visitors through the House of the Future exhibit. "I got—"

"Ooh! Business!" The Joker repeated as he rushed toward Valestra. "Sounds like fun!" He grabbed Sal by the collar and dumped him into the tiny car. "Come," he said gleefully, "we'll repair to more comfortable environs." He hopped into the seat next to Sal. "Now hold on to those hats and glasses," he grinned. "There's a teeny little bit of a jump at first." The tiny car took off like a shot, sailing along its track faster

than a roller coaster toward the House of the Future.

Sal Valestra wasn't prepared for this abuse. As the car slowed to a halt inside the futuristic home, he clutched at his chest in pain. Meanwhile The Joker gaily leaped out of the car. "Honey, I'm home!" he shouted.

In response, a small mechanical dog appeared at The Joker's feet. As it yapped happily, The Joker viciously kicked it across the room. He smiled back at Valestra. "Don't mind my home security system," he grinned. "Can't be too careful with all those weirdos around."

Valestra followed as The Joker entered the Kitchen of the Future. There, a female robot with a knife in her hand endlessly chopped at invisible food. "What?" The Joker whined. "Meat loaf again? Aww, I had it for lunch!" The Joker affectionately placed his hands on the robot's shoulders and turned to Valestra. "Isn't Hazel here a cutie?" he asked. "True, she's a real homebody, but you can't help who you fall in love with!" When The Joker suddenly turned from his robot companion and walked into the living room, Sal followed.

"So," The Joker said as he sat down, "tell me what's on your so-called mind."

"It's Batman," Valestra answered, happy to be getting down to business at last. "He's gone nuts. First he whacked Chuckie Sol, then Buzz, and now he's after me! I know it! Couple of days ago," Sal wheezed, "I saw him spyin' on me, from the roofs!"

"Y'know," The Joker said thoughtfully, "I've been reading lately how old Guano-Man is wound tight enough to snap. Wouldn't it be great," he said gleefully, "if I've finally driven Batso off the deep end?"

"This isn't a joke!" Valestra shouted, beads of sweat forming on his brow. "Batman's knockin' us off and you're the only one who can take him down!" Valestra laid down his suitcase and opened it to show The Joker what was inside. "Five million dollars up front, with whatever you want to finish him off!"

The Joker sneered, unimpressed. "What do I look like, pest control?"

Now Valestra was really mad. "Think, you fool!" he shouted, flinging the suitcase to the ground. "Once he gets me, how long till he gets you?" He rose from the couch and moved toward The Joker. "You know what I'm talking about!" he growled, grabbing The Joker by his collar. "Your hands are just as dirty! Dirtier!!"

The Joker had a faraway look in his eyes as Valestra tugged on his jacket. Then his lips began to tremble, his eyes began to redden, and his nostrils began to flare. Watching this transformation, Sal Valestra had the sickening feeling he'd made a terrible mistake. "Don't touch me, old man," The Joker hissed as he rose to his feet and slapped Valestra's hands away.

Valestra cowered in fear. But The Joker suddenly smiled—as friendly and outrageous as he'd been just moments before. "I don't know where you've been!" he quipped.

Sal Valestra could only tremble in fear. "Oh, Sal," The Joker continued, "no one could take a joke like you. Of course I'll help you out!" he said as he hugged Sal lovingly.

"Really?"

"Certainly! No way is anybody gonna hurt my pal Sal!"

Sal Valestra began to smile nervously. He hadn't thought he could pull it off, but it looked like he had! He'd managed to enlist The Joker to get rid of Batman! As his smile widened, The Joker put a finger to the corner of Valestra's mouth, trying to coax a bigger smile out of the sickly old gangster.

"That's it, that's what I want to see," The Joker said, pointing to his own face as an example. "A nice big smile."

"I'm exhausted," Andrea Beaumont said as she unlocked the door to her hotel room. She turned to Arthur Reeves, her date for the evening. "Thanks for the dinner, Artie." She smiled.

Reeves stood by the door as Andrea opened it to reveal an elegantly furnished room. "You know," Reeves began, "it's not good to go to bed on a full stomach." He placed his hand over Andrea's. "We . . . could stay up," he suggested, as he brought his free hand up to her shoulder. "Talk for a while . . ."

Andrea turned away shyly. She really didn't want this. "Oh, Artie," she replied, "I've got a killer day tomorrow. The banks, the attorneys—" She glanced into the room. The terrace door was open, and the drapes blew lazily inside. She remembered closing the door before she'd left. Was it possible that someone was already inside waiting for her? And could it be . . . him?

Reeves was insistent on entering, but Andrea turned to him and smiled. "Call me—okay?" she whispered as she planted a warm kiss on Reeves's lips. Reeves's eyes opened wide—perhaps he was getting somewhere with Andrea after all. He smiled dreamily as Andrea closed the door for the night.

Andrea leaned against the inside of the door and sighed. She was relieved to be rid of Reeves. What a pompous pain he was. In the darkness, she walked toward a light and turned it on.

Andrea Beaumont registered no surprise when she saw Batman standing in the middle of the room. She looked at him coolly a moment, then turned and walked away. "Don't you ever knock?" she asked.

It was a funny, witty response, something Bruce Wayne would almost have expected Andrea to say. But Batman wasn't here to make small talk. Instead, he removed a photograph from under his cape and showed it to Andrea. "Have you ever seen this?" he asked.

Andrea glanced up at the picture. "No," was all she said.

Batman thought that was unlikely. "But that's your father. He's the one who set up their corporate partnership."

"So? That's his job."

Batman pressed forward. He had a strong hunch about this case, and ten years of detective work proved he was usually right about these things. "He was the one element that tied these gangsters together," he said emotionlessly. "Where's your father now?"

"Haven't a clue," Andrea said nonchalantly. "He's

a world traveler, remember? Why don't you try Madagascar?"

"That's not what you told Reeves," Batman responded. "You told him you were closer than ever to your father."

Andrea was furious. "You had me bugged, is that it?"

"I can read lips."

"Then read them now. Get out."

Underneath his costume, Batman's heart was aching. The last thing in the world he wanted was to hurt the one woman he loved as much as life itself. He couldn't go on with this. He shook his head sadly and turned to leave. But as he stood by the terrace door he turned back to look at Andrea. He had to try one last time. "Why won't you tell me where he is?" he asked. "Are you still following his orders?"

His words stung Andrea, bringing back unhappy memories of the last time she'd seen Bruce Wayne. "The way I see it," she sneered in response, "the only one in this room controlled by their parents is you."

It's over, Batman thought. *No one I ever loved could say something like that.* Without another word, he stepped out onto the terrace and disappeared into the night.

Andrea Beaumont locked the terrace door, then sat down on the side of her bed and wept.

CHAPTER 10

A single light glowed in a window of Sal Valestra's brownstone later that night as the shadow of Phantasm fell across the town house's face. A misty cloud gathered near one of the darkened, barred windows for a brief instant, but as the window was flung open, both cloud and Phantasm disappeared.

Inside Valestra's home, Phantasm wandered through the darkened corridors in search of its latest victim. But Valestra wasn't hard to find—all Phantasm had to do was follow the sound of his wheezing, raspy breath.

Phantasm gently pushed open the door to Valestra's study. There, in the center of the room, was Phantasm's prey. He sat in his easy chair, legs up, his face hidden behind the day's newspaper, wheezing and gasping, unaware that he was about to meet his angel of death.

Phantasm entered, lifting an arm to reveal the razor-sharp hand blade. Phantasm towered over Valestra—but Valestra simply continued wheezing as he read the paper.

Something is wrong here, Phantasm thought. Valestra was too . . . still. The old man hadn't moved an inch since Phantasm had entered the room. Phantasm lifted the hand blade, ready to strike, and yanked Valestra's paper away.

Sal Valestra was dead. His eyes were wide open and dry, and his mouth was twisted into an inhuman smile. On his chest, a tape recorder played a cassette of Valestra's painful gasps. Propped up next to the recorder was a remote-controlled radio-camera. Phantasm was stunned. This was some kind of trap. The camera suddenly turned and focused on the ghostly figure.

"Whoops!" The Joker said. His voice was coming from the camera's speaker. "Guess the joke is on me! You're not Batman after all! Looks like there's a new face in Gotham."

Phantasm started running as The Joker continued, "And soon his name will be all over town." He giggled. "Not to mention his legs, and feet and head—"

Phantasm leaped out the window of Sal Valestra's brownstone just as the building exploded. A cloud of smoke formed in midair, carrying Phantasm to a nearby rooftop. From there, Phantasm watched as the police and fire department arrived.

Phantasm was shaken. This was not in the plan. But at least Valestra was dead, and the mission was complete. As Phantasm prepared to leave the rooftop, glancing at the magnificent Gotham City skyline, it noticed a bat-shaped figure hurtling down from the sky. Instantly, a cloud of mist formed at Phantasm's feet, carrying the grim figure from rooftop to rooftop.

Batman swooped down low toward Phantasm, swinging into the cloud of smoke the dreaded avenger left behind as it attempted to escape. But this time there was no escaping. This time Batman was ready. Through the mist, he spotted the now-familiar silhou-

ette and knocked Phantasm to the ground. Phantasm tumbled, landing feetfirst, coming face-to-face with Batman.

Batman made the first move. He leaped forward, swinging at Phantasm. But Phantasm ducked out of the way and kicked Batman in the chest. Batman fell back and down, but as Phantasm towered over him, Batman swiftly swept his leg under Phantasm's feet. Phantasm fell to the ground.

"This madness ends now!" Batman shouted as he leaped toward Phantasm. But Phantasm's feet crashed into Batman's chest as he descended, flipping him over Phantasm and onto the ground. As he fell, however, Batman grabbed onto Phantasm's cape and quickly maneuvered the mysterious figure into a bear hug.

Just then, Batman heard the sound of an approaching helicopter. *The police,* Batman thought. *Can't tangle with them. Have to finish this before—*

WHAM! Phantasm had used the moment's distraction to elbow Batman hard in the stomach. Batman fell back, gasping for breath. When he stood up to face Phantasm again, a cloud of smoke was already forming around the villain. As the sound of the approaching helicopter grew louder, Batman leaped into the cloud to stop Phantasm.

Batman searched through the dense mist, but as the police helicopter came close, the smoke started whipping around the roof until it disappeared completely. As the copter hovered in the air next to Batman, he saw that Phantasm had gotten away. He hoped he would be as lucky.

"Batman!" the helicopter cop shouted over his bullhorn. "Stay right where you are." In response, Batman turned toward the edge of the building and leaped off.

"Stay on him!" the cop inside the helicopter told the pilot—but that was easier said than done, as Batman raced over the rooftops, jumping, dodging, and swinging off flagpoles.

Although it might have seemed to the helicopter cops that Batman was simply fleeing, he actually had a plan in mind. Each jump he made across Gotham City's caverns of steel brought Batman a bit closer to ground level. If he could get down to the street, he'd be able to escape. He spotted an eagle-shaped stone gargoyle down below and dived toward it. Landing safely, he scanned the area for his next drop. About twenty feet below him, he noticed a wide skybridge. That would do just fine, he thought.

Batman sailed to the ground, landing safely on his feet. From here it would be easy to—

"Freeze!"

Batman spun around. There, behind him, was Harvey Bullock, accompanied by about twenty of Gotham's Finest. Their guns were drawn and trained on Batman.

Warily, Batman stepped back—and flipped over the side railing of the bridge. Police guns blazed as

Batman dropped through space before landing with a grunt on the top floor of a construction site.

Batman peered over the edge of the half-completed building toward the ground below. Two dozen police cars and two SWAT (Special Weapons and Tactics) trucks carrying twenty men each were in the process of surrounding the building. To make matters worse, the helicopter was back, shining a spotlight on him. Batman knew he was in full view of all the troops down below.

As Batman raced from girder to girder to avoid the spotlight's glare, he noticed tanks of acetylene fuel tied to each beam. During the day, construction workers used the tanks for welding steel. At night, the tanks were roped to the girders for safekeeping. Batman realized how dangerous these tanks could be. If a stray bullet hit one—

Suddenly, shots rang out, and Batman ducked behind a packing crate, narrowly avoiding a hail of bullets.

On the ground below, Harvey Bullock arrived on the scene just in time to see the SWAT team prepare to flush Batman out of the construction site. Two of the men loaded tear gas grenades into their launchers and fired. The grenades left a trail of smoke as they shot high into the air before landing amid the girders.

Inside the construction site, Batman leaped out of the way of the oncoming grenades. It seemed as though dozens of them were raining all around him and filling the air with dense green smoke. He reached into his utility belt and put on a gas mask. Now the gas wouldn't affect him, and the smoke would give him enough cover to avoid being seen by the helicopter hovering nearby. When he thought the coast was clear, he ran.

On the ground below a SWAT team officer spotted Batman's cape fluttering past a beam. He raised his rifle and started firing. Batman ducked for cover as bullets ricocheted all around him. He was pinned down and couldn't move. Then, from the corner of his eye, he noticed one of the acetylene tanks nearby. Bullets were zinging all around the construction site. It was only a matter of time before—

BWOOOM! The tank exploded, hurling metal, wood, and a huge ball of flame through the air. Batman was blown back with the blast and knocked unconscious by a chunk of flying debris.

Moments later, Batman awoke. He was hurt. Badly. A wooden sawhorse had crashed onto his back in the explosion, and he pushed it off his body with a grunt of pain. He had begun crawling through the wreckage when he heard someone approaching. He gazed around and spotted a SWAT team moving through the ruins nearby. But from the randomness of their movements, Batman bet they didn't know where he was . . . yet. So he crawled behind a beam and waited, hoping they wouldn't spot him. In this condition, he could offer little resistance.

But it wasn't over yet. After a few moments, a spotlight shined on Batman. He looked up. The helicopter had spotted him again, and now it had him in its sights.

Batman reached into his utility belt and removed his grappling gun. It was a long shot, he knew, but this might be his only chance. He fired the gun at the helicopter, and the rope wound around the copter's landing wheel. The cop inside the copter looked stunned for a moment, uncertain of what was going to happen next. Then he gave the order to his pilot to pull out.

But when he did, he discovered a caped figure was hanging onto the other end of the rope. As the copter flew off, it was taking Batman with it! "He's climbing on!" the helicopter cop radioed in just before he began firing at Batman.

From the ground, the SWAT teams and cops saw Batman flying through the air and began firing. Bullets ripped through the figure hanging from the helicopter. Pieces of cape and cowl blew away, leaving the costume in tatters and revealing to the police below—

—a *sawhorse.*

The cops were furious! They'd been had by Batman—*again!* While they were busy shooting a piece of wood, Batman had probably already escaped! They raced around the back of the building, hoping they hadn't already missed their chance.

High up inside the construction site, Bruce—without Batman's cape and cowl— planned his next move. He was weak and dizzy from his ordeal. And now, if he was even seen close enough for someone to tell who he really was, his crime-fighting career would be over.

While the police and SWAT teams raced up the rear of the building, Bruce staggered over to the front. There he grabbed a crane cable that extended from the roof of the building all the way to the ground. Holding on to it with both hands, he pushed off and began sliding down.

Before he could reach the end of the cable, he spotted Harvey Bullock pointing at him from the ground below. "You! Stop!" Harvey shouted. In response, Batman leaped from the cable and hit the ground running.

Harvey and his men chased Bruce on foot. Soon they were joined by the SWAT team. Moments later, a police car picked up the pursuit. To Bruce, it seemed as though all of Gotham City was after him. As he ducked into a grimy alley, he felt as though he were being hunted down like a dog. *Why was he doing this?* he wondered. He risked his life fighting crime, and this was the thanks he received? Did anyone care whether he lived or died?

The other end of the alley was blocked by a wire fence. Bruce leaped at it with all his remaining strength and, as the police gained on him, managed to crawl over and fall to the other side.

On the street at the end of the alley, a car was waiting, its motor idling. As Bruce came closer, he saw the driver: it was Andrea!

"Get in," she said urgently. "Hurry."

Bruce tumbled into the backseat just as the police cleared the fence behind him. They could only watch as Bruce and his accomplice roared off into the night.

Lying in pain in the backseat of the car, Bruce managed a weak smile. One thought kept running through his mind: *Someone cared.*

"There are certain advantages to having a sturdy cranium, Master Bruce," Alfred said as he placed a bandage around Bruce's forehead. "But then, hard-headedness was always your virtue."

Bruce smiled as his butler finished taking care of his wounds and left the room. Then Bruce turned to Andrea, who had driven him from the alley back to Wayne Manor.

"You have an excellent sense of timing," Bruce said.

"It was all over the TV," Andrea explained. "I had to do something—"

"I'm grateful, of course," Bruce said. "But I still need to know why you're not telling me the truth about your father."

Andrea sighed, then reached down into her purse to remove the photograph Batman had left with her earlier. "Well," she said, as she handed him the photo, "I suppose the World's Greatest Detective will find out eventually. You remember Daddy was having a meeting that night with his partners . . ."

Bruce remembered. In his mind's eye he saw Andrea walking up the stairs to her home and waving good-bye to him. Then she opened the door and went inside. That was the last time he'd seen her until recently. Now he would discover what went on behind closed doors on that fateful day . . .

CHAPTER 11

Ten Years Ago.

Andrea Beaumont walked past the Tall Man without so much as a glance in his direction. The Tall Man winked at Andrea and smiled slyly. But Andrea paid no attention to him as she entered her home and shut the door behind her.

As she walked past her father's study she heard voices—angry voices. Instead of going up to her room as she'd planned, she lingered outside the study door.

"It ain't right, Carl," Chuckie Sol said. "You're a businessman, you know that."

"You've taken what's ours," Buzz Bronski added. "You're going to pay one way or another."

Andrea was horrified by the threat. She opened the study door and ran into the room. "Leave him alone!" she shouted.

Buzz Bronski, Chuckie Sol, and Sal Valestra turned.

"I'm sorry you had to see this, Ms. Beaumont," Valestra said through a cloud of cigar smoke. He waved a finger toward Bronski, who stepped forward and grabbed Andrea roughly.

"Let her go!" Carl Beaumont suddenly shouted. The sight of his daughter being pawed by the gangster was too much for him. He moved forward, but Chuckie Sol pushed him back. Beaumont dropped to his knees before Valestra, who smiled at the sight. "Please, Sal," Beaumont begged. "Give me one more day. I swear I'll get the money!"

Valestra flicked cigar ash onto the ground. "Convince me," he grunted.

"This time tomorrow," Beaumont pleaded. "On my mother's grave. As soon as the European banks open I'll have the whole amount wired to you."

Valestra thought it over a moment. He looked at Chuckie, who nodded yes. He glanced at Buzz, who winked okay. He took a long puff of his cigar and blew the smoke in Beaumont's face. Then Valestra leaned in close, so that his face was right next to Beaumont's.

"Twenty-four hours," he hissed. "This time tomorrow, we'll have our money . . . or I'll have your heart in my hand." Then he stood and, motioning for the other gangsters to follow, left Carl Beaumont alone with his daughter.

Carl Beaumont kneeled on the floor, sobbing softly, as Andrea rushed over. "Dad—are you all right?" she asked.

Beaumont looked at her through tear-streaked eyes. "Pack a suitcase," he said desperately. "We've got to get to the airport now."

"What?" Andrea said, stunned. "But you said you'd have the money—"

"It's not that simple," Beaumont mumbled as he tore through his file drawers, placing selected folders into a briefcase. "The money's tied up in investments. Could take weeks to free it up."

"But I can't leave!" Andrea protested. "Bruce proposed to me! We're going to be married!"

Beaumont grabbed his daughter by the shoulders and held her hard. "Listen to me," he shouted. "I just used up the last shred of pity Sal Valestra has! If I don't pay him back within twenty-four hours they'll find us—and they will kill us both!"

Tears welled up in Andrea's eyes as she pulled free of her father's grasp. "How—why did you do this, Dad? Why'd you get involved with these people?"

Carl Beaumont looked at his daughter and began to cry. He put his arms around her and hugged her close. "I'm sorry, Andi," he sobbed. "I—I just wanted a chance for you—I—" He swallowed hard, a grim determination building inside him. "I'll get you out of this. Somehow, we'll be free of those guys, whatever it takes. That's a promise."

CHAPTER 12

"We hid all over Europe," Andrea continued. Bruce winced with pain as he laid the old photo of Carl Beaumont and the gangsters on his desk. "Eventually we settled on the Mediterranean coast. Dad was able to parlay the money he'd embezzled into a fortune. Finally he had enough to pay them back . . . or so he thought. It would never be enough," Andrea said angrily. "They wanted interest compounded in blood. He had to find another way."

Bruce looked at her intently. "The man in the costume . . . your father?"

Andrea cast her eyes to the ground. "He said he'd get them. Somehow, when I heard about Chuckie Sol . . . well, I had to come back to find him . . . to stop him." Andrea reached for her purse and got up to leave. "I'm sorry, Bruce," she said. "That's twice I've come into your life and screwed it up."

Bruce caught and held her arm tightly. She turned to face him but couldn't look into his eyes. A single tear formed on her lower eyelid, and Bruce gently wiped it away. When Andrea looked sadly up at Bruce, the two embraced.

The next morning, Bruce awoke to find Andrea sitting on the porch, looking over the Wayne Estate. She seemed especially beautiful out there, Bruce thought, her hair blowing in the breeze, sunlight splashing across her face. He stepped out on the porch and wrapped his arms around her.

Andrea turned to face him. "Can we make it work this time?" she asked.

"I want to say yes," Bruce answered. "But you know it's going to come down to what happens between me and your father."

"Daddy doesn't matter anymore," Andrea said sadly. They held each other in silence.

Later, Bruce saw Andrea off. She had to be back in Gotham for some meetings but promised to return that evening. Bruce kissed her good-bye and smiled as she waved and drove off.

Alfred appeared at the manor's front door as Bruce entered. "It's good to see you and Miss Beaumont together again," he said, following Bruce inside. "Might one ask what this bodes for your alter ego?"

Bruce's shoulders slumped as he entered Wayne Manor's study. "I'm not sure, Alfred," he said. "So much has changed."

"You still love each other," Alfred said, more a statement than a question.

"It's true," Bruce agreed. "I love her." He raised his eyes to the portrait of his parents above the fireplace. "Maybe after this is settled," he mused. "Maybe then—"

"I'm sure they would have wanted you to be happy, sir," Alfred said.

Bruce nodded in agreement as he sat down behind his desk to examine the photos scattered there. A photo of him and Andrea from ten years before. A photo of his parents. So many memories . . . and among all the other photos was the one he'd taken from Valestra's house . . . the one of Carl Beaumont and his gangster associates.

Three of the four partners pictured were dead. The fourth, Carl Beaumont . . . well, Bruce would soon be meeting up with him.

And then there was the Tall Man with the sharp features in the background behind Sal Valestra. Bruce knew he had been Valestra's personal bodyguard. But why did he look so familiar?

"Is something wrong?" Alfred asked as he watched Bruce stare intently at the photograph.

"Maybe," Bruce murmured. He reached over to a cup filled with colored pencils and picked out a red one. He drew an upper lip on the Tall Man and frowned. Then he drew another line, a lower lip. Together, the two lines formed a grotesquely large, blood-red mouth over the face of the Tall Man.

"Oh, no!" Bruce exclaimed in horror as he gazed at the doctored photograph. The Tall Man was . . . The *JOKER!*

"You're telling me there were four precincts on Batman's heels and he still got away?" Councilman Reeves shouted into the telephone in his City Hall office the next day. The officer on the other end of the line tried to explain. There was so much confusion: the explosion, the sawhorse decoy, the chase through the alley . . .

But Reeves wasn't hearing any of it. He slammed the receiver down angrily. "Unbelievable," he muttered to himself as he stared down at his desk.

"Tsk, tsk!" a sly, hysterical voice said from behind. "And to think our tax money goes to pay those jerks!"

Reeves turned toward his office's private entrance. There, in the shadows of the doorway, stood a tall man wearing a hat and holding a cane. After a moment the tall man stepped from the shadows and into the light. It was The Joker. He smiled slyly when Reeves recognized him.

"You!" Reeves shouted in fear as he turned to flee through the main office doors on the other side of the room. The Joker pointed toward the doors with his cane and smiled. "That's right, Artie. Bring in the press, why don'tcha?"

Reeves began to turn the doorknob to do just that—but then he stopped. "Sure," The Joker giggled. "What a photo opportunity! The councilman and his wacky friend!"

Reeves took a deep breath as he turned to face The Joker. "You're no friend of mine," he declared.

The Joker's smile faded, as though he'd been insulted. "Oh, Artie," he said sadly. "I'm crushed! How the high and mighty forget!"

Reeves looked at him curiously. *What was this maniac talking about?* he wondered—but when The Joker opened his blood-red lips to speak again, the councilman knew exactly what it was.

"Don'tcha remember?" The Joker pleaded as he walked behind Reeves's desk and plopped down in his chair. "You, me, Sallie and the gang!"

"I never met them or you!" Reeves insisted as he

watched The Joker lift a letter opener off the desk and begin balancing it on his fingertips.

"Oh, but you knew about it afterward," The Joker sneered. "And put it to good use, eh?"

Reeves bowed his head. There was no getting out of it now. The Joker knew the whole story. "What do you want?" he asked as he looked up at The Joker.

"To find out who iced the old gang!" The Joker screamed as he stabbed the letter opener into the desk. Reeves quivered as he tried to calm The Joker down.

"Haven't you read the papers?" he said. "It's Batman!"

The Joker opened his hand to reveal a joy buzzer strapped to his palm. He pressed the button and wagged his finger at Reeves. "Ennnnh! Wrong! It ain't the Bat. Nope nope nope!" he insisted, shaking his head furiously. "I seen the guy—he looks more like the Ghost of Christmas Past, nowhere near as cute as Bat-boy."

Reeves couldn't believe it. He'd been absolutely sure—but how could he trust the word of a crazy man like The Joker? "You're saying it's someone else?" he asked.

"Yeah," The Joker answered. "Someone who wouldn't mind seeing our old pals out of the way. Maybe"—his eyes suddenly widened with terror—"me too!"

An evil smile rose to The Joker's lips as he watched Arthur Reeves's discomfort grow. "That's when I thought about you, Arthur," The Joker said. "An important, upstanding guy like you could find it awkward if certain secrets were revealed about your past."

"Wait. You're not saying that I—" Reeves began, but his words were cut short by the sound of his secretary on the speakerphone.

"Mr. Reeves?" the tinny voice said. "Miss Beaumont on the line."

The Joker's eyes lit up with glee. "Beaumont?" he whispered as he turned toward Reeves. "Not the babe?! Oh, you devil you." The Joker grinned slyly, then reached over to the telephone and pressed the button that would connect the call.

"Arthur?" Andrea Beaumont's voice suddenly came over the speakerphone. Reeves attempted to lift the receiver to keep the conversation private, but The Joker pushed him away from the phone and lifted a finger to his lips. This was one conversation he wanted to hear.

"Hello, Andrea," Reeves said uncertainly, his eyes darting back and forth from The Joker to the telephone. "We're still on for lunch, right?"

"I'm sorry," Andrea replied. "I got hung up. I'll explain everything tonight, okay?"

Reeves looked at The Joker. What did he want him to say? The Joker nodded. "All right," Reeves said. "I'll see you then." At the instant Reeves completed his sentence, The Joker leaped toward the phone and

clicked it off. Then he turned angrily toward Reeves and grabbed him by the collar.

"Ain't that a co-inky-dink," The Joker said menacingly. "We're talkin' about the old man, and his daughter just happens to call."

Reeves backed away from The Joker, but the madman kept coming closer and closer, until the councilman had no place to turn.

"Makes you want to laugh, doesn't it, Artie?" The Joker sneered as a jet of green gas hissed from his joy buzzer into Reeves's face.

Yes, Arthur Reeves thought when his mouth began to tighten into a huge and terrible grin, *it does indeed*.

CHAPTER 13

The doctors at Gotham City General had never seen a case like this before. Although it was obvious to them that Councilman Arthur Reeves had gotten a dose of The Joker's Laugh Gas, they'd never seen such a severe case. Moments earlier, Reeves had been carried into the emergency room, kicking and laughing uncontrollably. Now, despite all efforts to knock Reeves out, he was still hysterical, tears of laughter streaming down his face.

"Councilman, please," one of the doctors exclaimed, "you've got to control yourself!"

"I'm trying, for God's sake!" Reeves hissed through gritted teeth, but he couldn't help himself. The laughs just kept coming. Reeves felt his head start to ache, his heart start to pound. His body couldn't take much more of this, he thought. But it was just too funny for him to stop.

Then the doctor stepped in with a syringe and injected Reeves with something that made the laughter suddenly stop. "There," the doctor said as Reeves looked at him gratefully. "That should relax you enough for the toxin to run its course." He gently pushed Reeves back onto the bed. "Now," he said, "try to stay calm."

"Okay, okay," Reeves muttered as he slowly drifted off to sleep.

Five minutes later, Arthur Reeves's eyes popped open. Someone was in the room with him. A shadow by the window. *Was it The Joker,* Reeves wondered, *coming back to finish the job*?

No, Reeves realized as his eyes focused on the grim figure moving toward him. *It was worse than that.*

"Why did The Joker meet with you?" Batman asked, a hint of anger in his voice.

Although he was terrified, Reeves felt a smile rising to his lips. He tried to speak, but all he could do was giggle.

"It has to do with the gangster murders, doesn't it," Batman said, pointing an accusing finger at Reeves.

"He thinks you're involved." Batman's temper flared. "Why?!" he shouted angrily.

Reeves fought the impulse to laugh and slowly, haltingly, managed to speak. "I don't know," he began—and then started laughing again.

Batman had had enough. He grabbed Reeves by his hospital gown and yanked him forward. "That's not the answer I want," he said sternly. He meant business.

In response, Reeves's smile disappeared. "Beaumont needed me to help him and his kid get out of town," he admitted. "He kept in touch while they hid in Europe."

"When was the last time you spoke to him?"

Reeves ran his hand through his hair as he fought the returning giggles. "Years ago," he tittered. "Right before he refused to lend me money for my campaign. Sol and his pals said all they wanted was their money back, so I told them where Beaumont was hiding." Then, unable to control himself any longer, Reeves burst into hysterical laughter.

Batman had learned all he needed to know. As much as Batman wanted to punish Reeves, he could see that the corrupt councilman was already paying the price for his treachery. As Reeves twisted and turned in his bed, Batman opened the window and leaped off into the night.

Moments later Batman dropped onto Andrea Beaumont's hotel room terrace. He peered through the window to make sure no one was home before entering. Once inside, he walked across the room to the clothes closet and opened it.

Inside, Andrea Beaumont's clothes hung neatly on a rack, her shoes laid out in pairs on the floor. Nothing was amiss. Something Reeves had admitted made Batman think he would find something else here, but now he realized that he was too late. As he turned to leave, his eye caught a glint of metal on a nearby bureau. As Batman approached, he saw that it was a gold locket with a heart design on its face.

Batman lifted the locket and depressed a button to open it. Inside was a photograph, taken ten years before, of a younger Bruce and Andrea. *A picture taken in happier times,* Batman thought as he clutched the locket in his hand a moment before placing it back on the bureau.

Then the phone rang.

Batman lifted the receiver off the hook and waited to hear the voice of whoever it was on the other end of the line.

"Helloooo—anybody home?" The Joker asked. "Listen, Boopsie—even though you never call and never write, I still got a soft spot for you. So I'm sending you a few gifts—air mail. Oh, by the way," The Joker added, "I wouldn't recommend jumping out the window this time. Ta-ta, toots."

The window? Batman thought. He looked toward it—to see a miniature autogyro heading directly toward the hotel room. He remembered the tiny autogyros from the Gotham World's Fair of a decade before, how they playfully buzzed over Bruce's and Andrea's heads during some of their best moments together. But there was something attached to the bottom of this autogyro . . . something that looked suspiciously like—a bomb!

Batman dropped the phone and reached into his utility belt to remove one of his Bat-stars. With pinpoint accuracy he threw it toward the autogyro, now only a hundred feet from the hotel room window. Then Batman dropped to the ground.

The autogyro exploded on impact with the Bat-star, sending shards of glass and debris sailing through the room. As the dust settled, Batman could hear The Joker's voice, laughing hysterically on the other end of the telephone line. "Hello? Hello?" The Joker howled. "Operator, I believe my party's been disconnected!"

Not quite, Batman thought as he rose to his feet and quietly stepped out of the hotel room. Thanks to The Joker's overconfidence, Batman knew where the Clown Prince of Crime was calling from. He intended to make good use of that information—to stop The Joker cold.

CHAPTER 14

E ight Years Ago.

Andrea Beaumont walked up the quaint stone path to the modest country home she and her father had rented. At first she had thought she would miss life in Gotham City, but she had been pleasantly surprised. She had grown to love living on the shores of the Mediterranean Sea. Life was so simple here. No parties to throw, no meetings to take. Everything moved so slowly here, everyone was so relaxed. It was wonderful. There was only one thing missing from her life . . . and his name was Bruce Wayne.

But now it was only a matter of weeks before she'd be reunited with the man she loved. After two years, her father had managed to put together the money he needed to pay back Sal Valestra and his other "partners." Daddy had wired them the money plus interest and announced that the two of them would be returning to Gotham within the month. Their ordeal was over; now Carl and Andrea Beaumont could get back to the business of living.

Or so Andrea thought as she walked up the steps to the house, a bag of groceries in her arm. With her free hand she reached for the doorknob. But before she could touch it the door opened as if by itself.

And on the other side of the door, on his way out, was the Tall Man. Andrea jumped back, startled by this face from the past, the bag of groceries falling from her hand. The Tall Man smiled as he stepped toward Andrea.

"But—but he paid you," Andrea cried out as the Tall Man, without saying a word, walked past her. She watched him for a moment as he descended the stairs, stopping to pick up an apple that had rolled out of Andrea's grocery bag. Andrea turned away as the Tall Man looked up at her and smiled, the terror inside her growing. He had found them . . . after all this time. What did it mean? What could he have done to—

Andrea gasped. "DAD!" she shouted as she ran inside the house and opened the door to her father's study.

Outside, the Tall Man crunched on his apple as Andrea Beaumont wept.

CHAPTER 15

Andrea Beaumont would never forget what she saw on that day eight years ago. At that moment she had made a silent vow, to herself and to her father, that she would never rest until the people responsible paid for their sins . . . with their lives.

Soon, her mission would be complete.

Inside the Home of the Future exhibit, The Joker was just settling down for dinner. With his trusty robot companion's chopping assistance, The Joker had cut a few slices off a huge slab of bologna. He was busy munching away when he noticed a breeze blowing in from outside. He walked to the front doors just in time to see the wisps of smoke come together to form a huge cloud in the middle of the Home of the Future. And then, from out of the clouds . . . stepped Phantasm.

"Joker—your angel of death awaits," Phantasm said.

"I'm impressed, lady," The Joker answered. "You're harder to kill than a cockroach on steroids."

Phantasm stood for a moment before slowly removing the skull-like mask that had struck fear into the hearts of Carl Beaumont's former partners.

"So, you figured it out," Phantasm said, revealing to The Joker that she was . . . Andrea Beaumont.

"Gotta hand it to you—nice scheme," The Joker said, slowly edging his way toward Andrea. "Costume's a bit theatrical, but hey, who am I to talk?"

Suddenly, The Joker threw a punch toward Andrea. But she ducked out of the way, raising her open hand to The Joker's face. A jet of smoke streamed out of her palm, covering The Joker's head. The Joker staggered backward, the smoke clinging to his head, as Andrea raised her hand blade to strike.

But the smoke cleared before Andrea could attack. The Joker grinned menacingly. "I can blow smoke too, toots," he said as a jet of acid squirted from his lapel flower onto Andrea's hand blade. Before her astonished eyes, the blade began to melt until all that was left was a stump of hot metal goo.

As Andrea tried to shake the molten steel from her hand, The Joker made his move. He punched her once, twice, three times, until she fell to the ground. The Joker attempted to pin Andrea down, but she still had plenty of fight left. She kicked the Clown Prince hard on the chin, sending him flying backward. As he scrambled across the floor of the futuristic home, Andrea stood.

"You're not smiling, Joker," she hissed. "I thought you found death amusing."

"Me?" The Joker asked innocently as he backed toward the robot companion who continued chopping at the slab of bologna. "Oh, no. You won't hear a giggle out of me," he said as he depressed a button on the robot maid's side.

The robot suddenly turned toward Andrea with its chopping blade swinging through the air. She ducked out of the way and kicked the robot to the ground. But with Andrea's attention focused on the robot, The Joker had a chance to make his next move. He grabbed a deadly looking power mixer and charged toward Andrea.

Again, Andrea easily managed to disarm The Joker and with a kick sent him crashing back against the table. Now it was her turn to attack. Grabbing The Joker by the collar, she raised her fist—and was stunned when The Joker reached over his head, grabbed the huge slab of bologna, and whacked Andrea over the head with it.

As Andrea staggered backward, The Joker raced toward the window. Andrea might have looked like a pretty young woman, but she fought as hard as Batman himself. If The Joker hoped to win, he'd have to take the battle outside as soon as possible.

The quickest way to do that was to crash headfirst through the House of the Future's picture windows. The Joker fell through the sky but landed on his feet and ran toward the main plaza to hide among the other abandoned exhibits in the Gotham World's Fair. By the time Andrea got to the window, The Joker was nowhere to be seen.

A cloud of smoke appeared, quickly surrounding Andrea. The cloud flew through the window and came to rest in the center of the plaza, in front of the Future of Technology exhibit's massive turbine fan engine. When Andrea stepped out of the cloud, she heard The Joker's voice.

"Well, if it isn't Smokey the Babe!" The Joker smirked. "Just in time for her biggest fan!"

Andrea looked at the turbine engine before her. The fan blades had begun to move! Andrea summoned a smoke cloud to get her away from the turbine, but the fan blades sucked the smoke away before a cloud could form. Andrea turned to run but found that the pull of the rapidly spinning fan was too great. Instead of moving forward, the turbine was sucking her back toward the deadly blades.

As the turbine reached its maximum speed, Andrea

felt her feet lift off the ground. Before she knew what was happening, she was flying toward certain death. But as she hurtled through the air she spotted what might be her only chance for survival: a metal beam from one of the other exhibits stood directly in between her and the turbine.

As she flew past the beam, Andrea reached out and grabbed it. But the pull was too great. Her hands slipped off the beam, and she flew ever closer to the spinning blades.

Her last chance was up ahead. Just a few feet in front of the turbine blades stood a flagpole. It was bent from the suction of the fan, but it held to the ground. If Andrea could only grab it—

Yes! But now she had run out of luck. Now she hovered mere feet from the turbine, hanging onto the pole by her fingertips. She estimated five minutes before her fingers could no longer take the strain and would let go.

The Joker gave her less, as he clicked the turbine controller into overdrive, making the blades spin even faster. Andrea screamed in agony as she struggled to hang on, but deep inside she knew that it was all over—

—until Batman showed up on his Batcycle. He'd spotted Andrea from the other end of the park and kicked his cycle into high gear, steering it toward the turbine. Faster and faster Batman drove toward certain doom. As the cycle got close to the turbine, the suction was so great the cycle actually lifted off the ground.

And that was Batman's cue. At the last possible second he leaped off the bike, sending it into the whirring metal blades. The cycle hit the turbine with a deafening crash, and the blades were twisted to pieces as they ground against the steel cycle parts. A moment later, the turbine ground to a halt.

As The Joker fled deeper into the fairgrounds, Batman confronted Andrea. "Your father's dead, isn't he?" he stated. "You came into town early to get Chuckie Sol, so you could shift the blame to your father if you had to."

Andrea nodded. It was all true. "They took everything, Bruce. My dad. My life. You. I'm not saying it's right, or even sane, but it's all I've got left." She raised her chin defiantly. "So either help me or get out of my way."

Batman raised a fist before her. "You know I can't do that," he said.

Andrea was outraged. "Look what they did to me," she exclaimed. "What we could have had! They had to pay!"

Batman shook his head sadly. "But Andi," he reasoned, "what will vengeance solve?"

"If anyone knows the answer to that," Andrea answered, "it's you."

Batman stared at her. She'd never understand that their goals were totally different. While Andrea was

looking for revenge, Batman was looking for justice. *They were so alike,* he thought, *yet so different.* And in that moment, Batman understood why he and Andrea Beaumont could never be together.

"Leave, Andi," he said. "Leave now."

Andrea looked at him coldly for an instant. Then the mist appeared, enveloping her. When the cloud cleared, Andrea Beaumont was gone.

CHAPTER 16

Now for *The Joker,* Batman thought as he searched through the fairground. He spotted the Clown Prince of Crime racing into the World of the Future exhibit and followed.

Inside, Batman was confronted with an astonishing sight: a miniature Gotham City, exact down to the last detail. Batman walked along empty miniature city streets and squirmed between dark, unlit skyscrapers barely eight feet tall. There was a replica of the Gotham skybridge up ahead. The real thing was twenty-eight stories high; Batman simply lifted his leg to climb over the miniature duplicate.

But as he searched through the city streets for his enemy, Batman didn't notice that one of the Gotham skyscrapers was *following* him. Batman did not know it, but The Joker was observing his every move. He had placed the upper half of one skyscraper over his head, using it to hide himself from Batman. And as Batman wandered through Gotham's miniature downtown area, The Joker pressed a button on his remote controller and stood back to watch the fun begin.

Batman first suspected a trap when the city suddenly came to life. Batman squinted from the skyscrapers' bright lights. They were as bright and busy as the real thing.

He saw the Gotham monorail cruising along its single track, watched miniature cars driving down miniature roads, heard miniature autogyros flying overhead, and felt the sting of their blades as they launched their attack.

Batman swatted at the autogyros and ducked out of their paths. As he twisted and turned, he noticed The Joker zipping across the city, riding on top of the miniature monorail. When the monorail passed over the Gotham River, The Joker leaped off. He flipped open the roof of one of the smaller buildings and hit a switch inside. Then he ran off, disappearing behind a block of skyscrapers.

Batman attempted to follow him but turned in pain as another autogyro buzzed him in the shoulder. He reached out to grab the first autogyro when another tore into his back. Batman looked around; the sky was filling up with the tiny helicopters—and one was diving right toward his face!

Batman swung his fist forward, smashing the auto-gyros to bits. Just as he destroyed what he guessed was the last of them, he saw an entire squadron of the tiny copters bank around a corner and head straight toward him!

Batman waited for the autogyros to swoop down close. Then, when they were almost upon him, he swiftly pulled off his cape, holding it open like a sheet in front of him. As the autogyros dived into the cape, Batman brought the ends together, creating a bag with the autogyros caught inside. Batman held on to the ends of the cape and heaved the sack of autogyros over his shoulder, smashing them to the ground. Then he swung his cape back over his shoulder, scattering pieces of the destroyed autogyros about the miniature street.

"You're too late, Batman," The Joker suddenly chuckled. Batman looked up to see The Joker as he shouted from atop the monorail that traveled past the miniature city. "There are twenty miles of tunnels under this place, and they're all filled with high explosives! In five minutes, everything goes up in the biggest blast since the asylum Christmas Party!" The Joker laughed crazily as he danced a little jig on the monorail track before racing out the exit.

Batman leaped from miniature building to minia-ture building until he reached the monorail exit. An instant later, he stood in the fair's main plaza area, scanning the grounds for any signs of The Joker. When Batman heard the slow droning sound of a rocket engine, he knew The Joker was at the Space Pavilion. Batman raced toward the huge stone statue of the waving astronaut that towered over the exhibit's entrance and spotted The Joker standing at the foot of the statue, wearing a futuristic rocket pack over his shoulders. Batman had to reach him before he took off. He ran as fast as he could, but he was too late. The rockets on The Joker's back flared red hot as The Joker rose into the sky.

But Batman wasn't ready to quit just yet. As The Joker hovered in the sky, Batman ran to the middle of the plaza, where the fair's centerpiece, a sculpture of a huge ringed planet next to a futuristic-looking rocket ship, rested. Batman raced toward the rocket— and continued running straight up the rocket's side before launching himself into the air. As The Joker slowly flew by, Batman grabbed him.

Hero and villain struggled in the sky, Batman attempting to hold on to The Joker and the jet pack while The Joker tried to shake Batman off his back and send him falling to his death. The Joker directed the rocket pack toward a bridge. As he flew under it, he suddenly jerked upward, smashing Batman's back against the underside of the bridge. The Joker was then able to flip the stunned Batman over so that he hung in space. But still Batman would not let go of The Joker.

"You just don't know when to quit!" The Joker said angrily as he tried to push Batman away. In response, Batman reached up with his free hand and punched The Joker hard, sending the two of them zigzagging wildly across the park.

The jet pack carrying the two enemies soared and fell through the sky, crashing through some exhibits while narrowly missing others. And all the while, the countdown to the destruction of the Gotham City fairgrounds continued.

"You're crazy!" The Joker protested. I'm your only chance to get out of here! Let me go or we'll both die!"

Batman snarled angrily. "That's the idea," he hissed, as he jerked The Joker's jet pack down, causing them to crash through the fair's huge ringed planet centerpiece. Batman and The Joker hit the ground at the same time; beaten and bloody, neither of them was in any condition to continue the fight. "For once," The Joker groaned, "I'm stuck without a punch line."

Then a shadow fell across The Joker's face. He looked up.

It was Andrea Beaumont.

Her face betrayed no emotion as she reached over and effortlessly lifted The Joker off the ground. The Joker was too weak to fight back. Instead, he raised his hands. "Okay," he said groggily, "I give up."

Andrea's expression did not change. It was as if

she hadn't heard a word of what The Joker had just said. "I surrendered already," The Joker said. "Tell her, Batman."

Batman staggered to his feet and started walking toward Andrea. "You've got to get out of here," he said. "This place is wired to explode."

Andrea's eyes narrowed as she glared at the helpless Joker. "No," she said. "One way or another, it ends tonight." Then she turned to Batman, and her expression softened. "Good-bye, my love," she said, and for an instant Batman remembered the Andrea he loved as much as life itself. He stepped toward her—

—and somewhere not too far away, Batman heard the dull thud of an underground explosion. It was quickly followed by another explosion. And another. And another. Each new explosion was louder than the one before. The Joker had set up a deadly chain reaction of explosions—and they were headed in this direction!

On the other side of the main plaza, Batman watched as the Ferris wheel suddenly blew off its supports and smashed through the monorail track. The wheel continued rolling forward until it crashed into the World of the Future exhibit. Then both exhibit and Ferris wheel blew to pieces.

An instant later the Gotham World's Fair centerpiece—the planet and rocket ship sculpture—exploded into a ball of white-hot flame. Still helpless in

Andrea's grip, The Joker started to giggle. Then his giggle grew into a chuckle. And his chuckle grew into a laugh. And his laugh grew into an insane cackle. He couldn't help himself. It was all just so darn *funny*.

Andrea looked down on The Joker as mist started billowing out around her. In a moment, a cloud had completely surrounded her and The Joker.

Batman staggered after them as The Joker's laughter faded away. "Andrea!!" Batman screamed.

But when the smoke cleared, both The Joker and the woman who had called herself Phantasm were gone.

As the Gotham City World's Fair collapsed, the ground below Batman's feet gave way. He plummeted down, down, down—until he splashed into one of the sewer tunnels under the city. The current carried him from one pipeline to the next, deeper and deeper into the system, eventually spilling him out into Gotham Harbor. His lungs close to bursting, Batman shot to the surface.

In the distance, the World's Fair exploded in a final display of fire and smoke.

CHAPTER 17

He was wounded, but he would survive, Alfred assured him back in the Batcave. Somehow, he always survived. But this time wasn't like the others. This time he'd left a part of himself back in the dying embers of the fairgrounds, a piece of his soul that was now forever lost. He carefully lifted the cowl away from his bruised face and put his head in his hands.

"I couldn't save her, Alfred," he sobbed.

Alfred placed a fatherly hand on his employer's shoulder. "I don't think she wanted to be saved, sir," he said. "Vengeance blackens the soul, Bruce. I always feared you would become that which you fought against. You walk the edge of that abyss every

Batman

night. But you haven't fallen in, and I thank heaven for that."

Bruce wasn't hearing him. He looked down at the ground in despair. Alfred kneeled before him to get his attention.

"Andrea fell into that pit years ago," he said. "And no one—not even you—could have pulled her out."

Alfred's words fell on deaf ears. Nothing the butler might say could ease Bruce's misery. The woman he loved was gone . . . and he could only blame himself. Bruce bowed his head sadly—and noticed something in the corner of his eye. Something—he couldn't tell what—seemed to be sparkling in the Batcave's dim light.

Bruce stood and looked at the glimmering light, his heart suddenly filled with hope "What is it?" Alfred asked. Deep inside, Bruce already knew, but he dared not say a word until he was sure.

He began walking, then trotting, then running at full speed across the bridge leading to the Batcave's entrance. In a moment he had arrived at the glittering light. He reached up into the darkness for it. Could it be? Could it—

It was.

Andrea's locket.

He knew there was only one way it could have gotten here. She had left it here, as if to tell him that she too had survived, but that their love had not. It could not.

Alfred peered thoughtfully at the morning paper's headline:

BATMAN INNOCENT

An out-of-focus photo of Phantasm's encounter with the late Chuckie Sol in the Shady Lady's parking garage filled most of the front page. "Well, thank heavens the public knows Batman was not responsible for Ms. Beaumont's deadly campaign," he said. "Apparently a *Gazette* reporter captured Mr. Sol's untimely demise on film."

Although Bruce appreciated his old friend's effort to change his mood, Alfred's observation could not break through the wall of emotion separating the two men.

Bruce Wayne stared at the locket tearfully. Although his sadness was still great, knowing Andrea Beaumont was still alive made it a sadness he could live with.

The passengers on the *Queen Elizabeth* luxury liner didn't need an excuse to celebrate. Every night was party night. The ship had left Gotham City two days earlier; there would be a total of fifteen more all-night celebrations before the ocean liner put into port.

One of the passengers, a friendly looking man, staggered along the deck, a glass of champagne in his hand. He'd left the party to come out here and toast the moon and the sky . . . and above all, the sea. He raised his glass up high—and noticed a lone woman standing on the far end of the deck, her hair and skirt blowing in the wind.

The passenger took his paper party hat off, smoothed back his hair, and with a confident yet slightly tipsy air, strode toward the mysterious woman.

"Quite a sight," he said as he stood by her side and gazed at the ocean.

"Yes," the woman said solemnly.

The passenger turned to look at the woman. Something in her voice made him feel concerned for her. "I'm sorry," he said. "Have you—lost someone?"

"Yes," Andrea Beaumont said.

Two days and a thousand miles away, a lone figure stood among the rooftops, his eyes closed, his mind lost in thoughts of what might have been and what could never be. There was an emptiness inside him, an emptiness he wasn't sure would ever go away. He had loved and lost, and he needed someone to fill the void. Someone to want him, someone to rely on him. Someone . . .

But as the Signal filled the nighttime sky, Batman put aside his thoughts and smiled.

He was needed.

About the Author

ANDREW HELFER was born and raised in Brooklyn, New York. Like Bruce Wayne, he was a child of privilege and attended prestigious New York City public schools. Later he went to college and did graduate work in journalism at New York University. Still later, he discovered the joy of comic books and has spent the last twelve years writing and editing them for DC Comics in New York. In his spare time, Andrew has written many illustrated children's books, branching storybooks, and novelizations, and working with fellow DC Comics editor Mike Carlin, he has coauthored fifteen episodes of the syndicated *Adventures of Superboy* television series.

Andrew lives in New York City. He has a cat named Roughhouse and one of the largest collections of Godzilla toys east of Tokyo.

THE NEVER-ENDING BATTLE
OF THE WORLD'S GREATEST
SUPER-HERO

For the first time ever you can get the
complete story all in one book!

Relive the events leading up to and following
Superman's epic battle with Doomsday. And
witness, at last, the ultimate fate of the
world's greatest super-hero.

Superman: Doomsday & Beyond
Louise Simonson
0-553-48168-1 $3.99/4.99 Can.